THE COPPER PEOPLE

BARBARA MARCH

SMART HOUSE BOOKS

SMART HOUSE BOOKS
100 Bain Ave., Toronto, on M4K 1E8
www.smarthousebooks.com

Publisher's Note: This is a work of fiction. Names, characters, places, and incidents are a product of the author's imagination. Locales and public names are sometimes used for atmospheric purposes. Any resemblance to actual people, living or dead, or to businesses, companies, events, institutions, or locales is completely coincidental.

BookCover Layout ©2017 Aaron Rachel Brown
Cover Art Patrick Hughes, photograph, Vancouver, British Columbia, 2016

printed in Canada
Printing Icon, Toronto, Ontario

The Copper People/Barbara March 1st ed.

ISBN 978-0-9689718-2-6

to those I have loved...

*"Non abbiate paura, il nostro destino
non può essere presa da noi, è un dono."*

*"Do not be afraid;
our fate cannot be taken from us;
it is a gift."*

Dante Alighieri, Inferno

ONE

....

I couldn't have known such a thing really existed, and never would have believed it, if it hadn't happened to me all those years ago.

It was when we had had enough of newness, open spaces, a dullness in life that was just plain predictable, that my husband and I decided to pack our bags and move somewhere else, where we would have to learn another language and understand a different culture. We had talked about visiting Italy years ago but with work and family there just never seemed to be time.

Never having visited Rome, the center of civilization, and being an ex-Catholic, I thought it would be the perfect place. We could have chosen Poland. Both my parents were Polish but they had never had passports and their land, which was now part of Lithuania and the Ukraine, had been expropriated at the beginning of World War II by the Russians who then promptly shipped them off to Siberia. And, since Poland was still under the yoke of communism, I didn't fancy trying to get into a country that agreed to the theft of my parents' lives and land and then said I needed a visa just to visit. No, that wasn't how I wanted to spend my 25th wedding anniversary.

"Somewhere warm," I said, and we found it. A very small, very beautiful hilltop village only a few hours drive from Rome.

The house we bought, sight unseen over the internet . .

something only a highly emotionally charged couple like us would do! . . had everything we thought we wanted, except an outdoor space. We would use it as a base and travel throughout Europe and so we thought we didn't really need one. You know, just lock up and go. But as we sat there on the *terrazza* of the café on our first visit to that little village my heart sank.

We had put a down payment on a beautifully restored, four-storey townhouse and now realized it sat right in the middle of a busy square. You could see the house from every angle. Not exactly a private little getaway. But as we sat drinking our delicious cappuccinos, waiting to meet the estate agent, neither one of us said a word. We both realized we had made a mistake but said nothing to each other. My husband looked at his watch and I knew it was time.

Montevecchio, I'll call it Montevecchio though that is not its real name, was a very old village. Apparently its history went back before the 6th century. At one time it was a thriving community with over nine thousand inhabitants but now there were only five hundred people living here, a veritable ghost town.

With no work after the Second World War hundreds of people left for the big cities or emigrated to America in search of a better life. Many of the landowners lost everything but there were a few noble families who managed to hang on to their estates and were now renting or selling them to the many incoming Germans and Brits who were cashing in on the rising equity of their homes in their own countries and wanted a little piece of the Italian sun. It was a working class town but it had all the amenities necessary to life without ever leaving it.

There was the café-bar, of course, in fact we eventually discovered there were three of them, a *'macelleria'* (butcher), a *'forno'* (bakery), an *'alimentari'* (grocer), even a dry-cleaners, as well as two supermarkets. So in many ways this town should have been perfect. But there was something odd about it, just a feeling I had that I couldn't really describe. It was typical for any *'stranieri'* entering any small Italian village to feel like they didn't belong, at least not at first, but no, it was something else. Something in their glances and whispers that made me feel uncomfortable. I put it down to my own overly sensitive nature.

"Good afternoon," the estate agent, Elena, greeted us warmly as we reached our home-to-be.

"Buona sera," we replied.

What was I doing? What were we thinking? Who was I going to talk to? I knew nothing of these people in this tiny village. I was a New World person! I had lived in a multicultural city filled with people from all over the planet. But here everyone was, well . . Italian! I wanted to run to my car and flee! Fly! But I just smiled, a sad longing smile in my heart, as I heard my husband say -

"I'm sorry. We don't speak Italian very well. But we will learn."

The agent smiled, which said to me, 'How sweet. How typical. These people come here and they can't even speak our language.'

"It is okay. I am learning my English. It is not good but I understand very well. You found the village well?"

"Yes. We came a little early and had a coffee at the bar there," Marshall said, pointing to the café.

I was sure that everyone in that café was watching us.

"It is a beautiful vista, no?"

"Oh, yes. Very beautiful!"

"Yes, a very old town. How do you say, strange also?"

"Strange?" I asked.

Just at that moment a little head covered with snow-white hair peeped out from a door only a few yards away and then disappeared. As I looked up the tiny street I thought how narrow it was, impossible for anything more than a scooter to pass through, but I was wrong.

"Where does that alley lead to?" I asked and within seconds a Mercedes wagon came hurtling down. I jumped back against the stone wall of the house. Elena gave Marshall a little push up on to the step by the door. The car literally had only centimeters to spare as it sped through. What was even more extraordinary was that it was filled with nuns!

"I am sorry. It is a little *pericoloso*."

No sooner had she said it than another car came roaring down.

"That road . . "

'More like a highway,' I thought.

"It goes to the old square. It is empty now except for another bar. This town has been unfortunate in the last years. Many people have left and not returned."

"Do you know this town well?" I asked.

"No, I have never been here before."

"Oh, now that is strange. Your office is not far."

"Yes, but Italians do not come here or buy here."

You can imagine this did nothing to calm my fears.

"It is time. I will ring."

She rang the little bell button but none of us noticed that another larger door next to us was wide open and a woman was suddenly standing there wearing a headscarf and apron. She was maybe in her fifties with a handsome face and bright black eyes.

"*Sera!*" she exclaimed and, after taking a long look at us, burst into tears! Even Elena was taken aback and the woman began speaking to her in rapid Italian as Marshall and I turned to each other doubtfully. Then, just as suddenly, the woman disappeared.

"Please, come in," said Elena.

When we entered the room behind the arched doors it was obviously the dining room and it was stunning.

"The lady of the house would like you to know that this room is original. The stone dates back to the 15th century. It was once part of a church, a small communal church which is now part of the house next door, you see it is above us, and this was the church crypt. You see up there," Elena pointed to a trap door in the center of the room, "That is where the dead were dropped."

"Bodies?" I asked.

"Yes, but it was long ago. You are not fearful?" she asked with a smile.

"Oh, no, no. Actually it's wonderful," I answered.

A crypt. How fascinating!

"If you will look up on the ceiling. There are painted symbols. Can you see?"

"Yes," Marshall and I said, both nodding.

The symbols were rather primitive but lovely in their color and simplicity.

"And now we see the house," Elena said, leading us out of the room.

"Marshall, wasn't that room beautiful?"

He nodded, giving me a little wink.

"The lady of the house is cooking you lunch so we will begin upstairs."

I whispered to Marshall, "Lunch?" He just shrugged his shoulders and we followed Elena up a small flight of stairs.

A young man, maybe around twenty, passed us in the narrow hallway. He wished us good afternoon and went into the kitchen. No doubt it was the woman's son. I was wondering why these people were selling. I asked Elena and she explained.

"They were all born in this village. Generations of their family lived here. But they would like to be near the coast, near the beach. They will be the first to go so far away but their son likes to windsurf."

Yes, well, why not? They move twenty kilometers away and it's the other side of world. We move over sixty-five hundred miles and don't give it a thought!

We turned to the right and went up a large stone staircase at the top of which was a high window open to the sunshine. As we got to this *finestra* the vista was staggering. I could see the whole countryside.

"If you look over there you can just view the sea," Elena pointed.

As we stretched out over the windowsill I got a bad attack of vertigo and moved back a little to let Marshall have a look.

"That is the Gran Sasso over there. It is one hundred kilometers."

She continued along the hallway but it was hard for Marshall to break away from the spectacular view.

"It is beautiful, isn't it?" I said.

He nodded silently, still gazing out the window.

"There is more beautiful vistas if you will follow me."

And we did and she was right.

"This is the living room or how would you call it . . studio? Study, maybe?"

A double set of French doors with matching shutters were open onto the two small Juliet balconies I had noticed from the café. From these you could see the bustling village and, beyond, the whole range of the Sibillini mountains still dusted with snow. Not only that, to the left of the doors was yet another tall window that opened out to the vista we had just seen. The light poured into the room. The ceilings were very high and there were some old architectural details and a lovely fireplace.

"The floor is original. They do not do this tiling anymore so the owners did not change it for new like the rest of the house."

'So far, so charming,' I thought but when I turned to Marshall his whole appearance had changed. He looked, well, a little puffed up, like a proud bird who was telling himself that maybe he hadn't been so crazy after all.

The agent showed us the second room on that level. It was the original kitchen and had a sink with running water but was filled with boxes now and was only being used as a *ripostilio*, a storage room.

"This would make a third bathroom," she said. "The owners were to do that if they stayed in the house. Please you follow, there are two more levels."

So on we went up another flight of stairs.

"Good exercise," I commented.

"Yes, it is, but maybe you are tired?"

"No, no, it's good for me."

We followed Elena to the next level.

"There are two bedrooms and a whole bathroom."

The first bedroom was very pretty. There was plenty of space for the queen-sized bed, two bedside tables, a large armoire and an antique chest of drawers. There were two large windows with shutters already open.

"Here you can see the mountains even more clear.

Beautiful, no?"

I nodded.

"You never see shutters in America."

"They are necessary here in Italy. At night we leave the windows open and close the shutters for coolness in the summer and they are good in winter too, they help keep heat inside."

Marshall looked out the window overlooking the central square and noticed something.

"Come here."

He motioned me to come closer.

"Marshall, you know I can't."

"Well, you'll have more problems than just looking out. The laundry line is right here."

"You're kidding."

I looked as far over as I could and, yes, that was where the laundry lines were but the washing machine was on the main floor! That meant three flights of stairs and hanging your body halfway out a window that was as high above the ground as a Magic Mountain ride! Impossible! But I didn't say anything.

We moved down the hallway to the bedroom next door. It was smaller yet still had enough room for a bed and an armoire. But the best part of all was the bathroom. It was grand. It had a spa tub, a separate shower, a beautiful commode with a sink built in, plus a bidet, something Marshall just loved. He thought they were a most excellent European custom. Good for the environment because you didn't need toilet paper and you could do a proper wash-up. I can tell what you're thinking but it's true.

"We are now up to the last level."

Elena started climbing up a small circular wooden staircase.

I was sure it would be just an attic, a storage place, unfinished and very tiny. But no, when we got to the top, although the ceiling was low, there was still enough room to stand up. The floor was tiled and there were two skylights on each side of the center beam.

"There is a view here too."

Elena pulled out a little stool and asked us to have a look out the skylight. I had to get on tippy-toe but she was right, now you could look over the rooftops at an even wider version of the panoramic skyline.

What could I say? I had fallen madly in love with the house. After a few moments of silence between Marshall and me, I asked him -

"Well, what do you think?"

"Amazing."

"Yes, but . . ""

"I need to look at it once more."

"We're buying it?""

"Well, we're here now. We've done it really, haven't we?"

"Yes, so?"

"But I'd like to look at it again on our own."

"So, this is all," continued Elena, "Except there is a room below the house that is part of it. It is a garage but not big enough for an auto. We shall see that at the end."

Marshall asked Elena if we could go through everything once more by ourselves.

"Well, I will ask the Signora."

The nagging feeling in the base of my belly had not completely gone away. The house was beautiful, the vista was indescribably beautiful and there was a lot of room for our 'desperate for an Italian vacation' friends and family. What was eating at me that I still felt we should not go through with it?

As we followed Elena back down to the main floor there were wonderful smells wafting up towards us. She must be cooking a four-course meal! Elena disappeared into the kitchen and we waited for her outside the front door. As I turned to have another look at the farmlands and mountains over the stone balustrade of the narrow road I could see from the corner of my eye the same white-haired woman peering through her window at me. I turned and she immediately closed the shutter.

Elena came through the door and joined us.

"Yes, it is all right."

As we began our tour again we bumped into what I knew had to be the husband. He was a thin wiry man, rather handsome and jocular. He spoke a little English and greeted us with -

"Welcome. It is a delicious house, yes?"

"Yes, very beautiful."

"Please to look, take your time and then we *mangia*," he said, putting his fingers to his mouth.

"Thank you," Marshall said and shook his hand.

It's no use going into any more details except to say that, of course, we decided to do it. But I had no idea then what this house would really cost us, in more ways than just money.

We all gathered in the kitchen, including Elena and the young man we had met earlier. Elena would now do the translating as we finalized the arrangements. There was just one little snag in the works. Something we didn't expect but then that seemed par for the course. The couple wanted to sell all their furniture. I mentioned to Elena that on the website it said that some of the furniture was included in the price. Elena translated and, without a second's pause, the Signora said firmly, *"Devono comprare tutto o niente."*

We didn't understand what she meant and looked at Elena with questioning glances. There was a pause, a long pause, then Elena spoke.

"I am sorry but she says you must buy all the furniture or you can have none of it."

I was stunned. Oh, oh. There went my stomach again. I knew we should have walked away when we had the chance. Actually we should never have walked in here in the first place and I should have told Marshall about my gut instinct. Now what were we going to do?

"They want twenty-five thousand euros."

What could we do? There was nowhere to have a private consultation and, I will regret this to my dying day, I hesitated just a moment too long and heard Marshall saying -

"Agreed."

Just like that! He didn't ask me or bargain or anything! He just agreed. Well, I can tell you that, besides me, another person was completely stunned and that was our estate agent. I could see on her face that she was thinking, 'This is not done in Italy! You must bargain, haggle, anything!' She couldn't speak. I looked at the Signora and her husband but they sat there quite calmly. I pulled Marshall's shirtsleeve and whispered to him as quietly as I could -

"What are you doing? It isn't worth that much."

He just waved his hand in front of my face, not condescendingly but as though he were saying, 'Trust me.'

Suffice it to say that lunch went on as planned. Elena was unable to stay and said her goodbyes. I'm sure she returned to her office in a state of shock. And yes, it was a four-course meal. We did our best to communicate in three languages. The husband, who worked on a fish boat that sailed around the coast of Africa, knew a little French and somehow we managed.

We had been staying at a lovely place not far away. It was a *comune* of little houses owned and run by a noble family. They had turned their grounds into a vacation retreat. It had two swimming pools and wonderful privacy but when we got back I still had this nagging fear and doubt. And besides the unexpected issue of the furnishings another serious problem came up that totally unsettled me.

Apparently it was customary in Italy, not lawful mind you, that you could declare any purchase price you wanted for the house you bought. What this means is, if, let's say, I was buying a house for two hundred thousand euros, the real value of the property and the price on the realtor's website, I could turn around and claim that I had only paid sixty thousand euros for it. Why you ask? It all came down to avoiding taxes. But the sticking point was that if I sold the property within the next two years, at the real value of two hundred thousand euros, then anyone who wanted to buy the property would not be able to get a mortgage or a loan from an Italian bank precisely because it was originally undervalued at sixty thousand euros which, in essence, is all it would be worth as far as the government and the bank were concerned. Someone could, of course, pay me my price and continue to under-declare the value themselves if they wanted to buy it with cash but how many people have that kind of money? And, to really confuse you, if I waited five years before I sold the house then I could sell it for the true value of two hundred thousand euros without paying any back taxes! So I told Marshall, before we do anything, we have to talk to a lawyer and that we should declare the full value no matter what because I had no idea if I wanted to stay in Italy that long. And this began another very strange journey through the machinations of

Italian property buying.

The lawyer's name was Flavio and we met him at the café across from his office in the historic city of Ascoli Piceno. He was tall and slender and swarthy-looking and very business-like, a little grim perhaps, but extremely courteous when he approached us and shook hands.

He immediately ordered coffee. His English was excellent which was a relief because I had no idea how we could make ourselves understood in Italian about something so complicated.

"So you have questions for me?"

He didn't beat around the bush.

"Well, yes, quite a few, and may I say thank you for agreeing to meet with us on such short notice and speaking such good English. Our Italian is, well, non-existent," Marshall said with a self-deprecating grin.

"Do not apologize. Most people who are buying are not Italian."

"Well, as you know, we are going ahead with the deal but there is something we came across which is giving my wife sleepless nights. It's this thing about declaring or not declaring."

"That is up to you. As you wish to do."

"Yes, but can you explain what it means exactly. We have nothing like that in America."

"It is simply a way for the Italians to not pay any more tax then they have to. We already pay too much."

"But is it legal?"

"In a way yes, in a way no."

"Oh?"

It was all I could say. The knot in my stomach was getting tighter.

"I will try to explain. If you declare the house under its value you will not be taxed so much by the government. If you declare the full value you will obviously be taxed on the full amount."

"I can see that but what is the purpose of it? The difference is minimal."

"Yes, but you will also pay the notary more, you will pay the property agent more and you will pay me more."

"And if we don't declare the full value?" I asked.

"You will pay everybody less."

This was getting us nowhere and Marshall asked -

"But won't the government know what we've done?"

"No, no, the government must not know what you have done."

"Excuse me?" I interrupted, "Then it is illegal."

"Yes and no."

Here we go again.

"We make no paper trail. We make sure that there is no evidence of how much the house really cost."

"But," I interrupted again, "That is impossible. It was on the website, the full asking price was on the agency website!"

"That does not matter. Just because that was the amount on the website does not mean you paid that amount and the government has no way of knowing what you paid."

When we heard that I knew there was no getting away with it.

"If you are concerned then you should just declare the full value. I am not allowed to advise you to under-declare. That would be illegal."

That clinched it for me. And then he added -

"Oh, and another thing. We must go to the bank. I have made the appointment. You must have an account with not only the amount you propose to pay but at least twenty thousand on top of that to show your good intentions."

"Can't we wire the money to their account? We did that with the deposit."

"No, it is not possible. They are not declaring the full value."

I sat dumbfounded.

"But we are!"

"Yes, and so there will be no problems it is best that you give them cash."

"And if we don't do that?"

"The Signora and her husband may not do the deal."

"Of course they'll do it."

"Can you be sure?"

"No, maybe not, but two hundred and forty thousand euros in cash?!" I exclaimed.

"No, not so much. It is very easy. They are declaring sixty thousand euros so we make six bank drafts of ten thousand and one for maybe three thousand for fees and taxes for the *notaio* and the rest you will pay in cash."

"But why?"

"So there is no paper trail."

I finally understood.

"The six bank drafts are okay for the amount they are declaring, is that it?"

"Yes."

I simply couldn't believe what I was hearing.

"Is this your advice?" added Marshall.

"Yes, it is the way we do it here and it is actually best for everyone."

So we kept Flavio's appointment at the bank. When he arrived he asked us to wait a moment while he had a word with the bank manager. We waited several minutes and then he returned.

"I am sorry but we cannot do it today."

"What's the matter? Didn't our money get transferred?" Marshall asked, looking concerned.

"Oh yes, your funds are here but the bank does not have enough cash in its vault."

Only silence prevailed, not a pause, just dumb silence.

"What do we do now?" I asked him.

"They will send from another branch tomorrow afternoon with the necessary euros and we will meet here then."

We agreed to return at one o'clock which surprised me because it isn't normally possible to do anything in provincial Italy between noonish and four since that's when they take their *pranzo* and siesta. One of many Italian customs that America should have adopted long ago. Imagine working from eight till half past noon, coming home to a three course meal prepared by a wife, or mother or grandmother, then reading the paper or a book which puts you into a lovely sleep for an hour, then waking to the smell of a robust coffee and back to work, finishing your day at eight in the evening and returning home again for a light snack and then a *passeggiata*, a leisurely promenade around the town. The people are satiated, rested and contented while we, on the contrary, priding ourselves as productive and efficient workers, get up at six in the morning, drive our children to school, drive ourselves in the worst traffic, praying we won't be late, work till one and then get half an hour to gulp down our food, fast food preferably . . who has time to go to a restaurant? . . then return to work and leave at five or six, pick up the kids from the much-needed after school program, dash home, put some muck together as quickly as possible, gulp that down, do the dishes and, if there's time, get the homework done, then get them to bed and finally fall asleep in front of the television. And God help us if we went for a nightly perambulate! We might get mugged or worse, someone might steal our children from their beds! Not very conducive to the digestion. I believe that is why the French and Italians live longer than we do. It's not just the olive oil, I'm sure.

At the bank the next afternoon the manager was ready with the six drafts and exactly the amount of cash that was necessary in thick bundles of five hundred euro notes. Thank goodness Flavio decided to take responsibility for it and put it in his safe.

Needless to say I had another sleepless night.

It was chilly for early June. As a matter of fact the entire time we had been in Le Marche it had been cold and rainy except for the day we saw the house. Was that a sign or what? What was my problem? I still couldn't shake the queer feelings inside me.

The next morning as we drove again to Ascoli it was overcast. I would have preferred a brilliantly sunny day. It might have cheered my spirits.

As we entered Flavio's office we were surprised to find the room jam-packed.

"Look at all the people!" I whispered to Marshall.

The Signora and her husband were standing in one corner of the room. Four people were moving an enormous table and eight chairs into the center. There must have been a dozen people there. In an American real estate deal there were only ever two or three people in the room, you, your lawyer and maybe the bank or the seller's lawyer.

Flavio came toward us looking very harassed.

"So sorry, we must set up first. Please just wait, we will

almost be ready."

"Marshall, what are all these people doing here?"

"I have no idea," he said with an odd smile as he watched the whole spectacle.

In only a few minutes everything was in place. Flavio told us to sit down in the chairs on either side of him. Across from us sat the Signor and Signora without a lawyer. At the head of the table sat the notary, impeccably dressed in a black suit with very wide lapels and sporting a large black ascot tie. At the other end sat the estate agents, Elena and Maria Luisa, and two other women but I had no idea who they were and, lastly, Flavio's secretary.

Flavio gathered up his papers and began the proceedings by introducing everyone. That's when I found out who the two extra women were. Apparently it was required by law that all contracts regarding the sale of property be written in Italian and also in the language of the buyer or seller if they are *stranieri* and that there must be bilingual translators in the room when the contracts are read aloud. It was normal to do this in both Italian and English and the two women were there to listen and to sign the final document to certify that both versions said the same thing. I found out later why the reading aloud was mandatory. It was done to protect those who might be illiterate. I thought that was marvelous but quite useless to the present Italians! They were literate! Unfortunately it was us, the Americans, who held the record for illiteracy, but I won't dally with politics and get on with the story.

We had never told Flavio exactly what we did for a living, not really. We said we were retired writers. Of what you ask? Well, we weren't retired writers though we had once collaborated on a few film scripts that got nowhere. We were retired entertainers. We were actors and my husband was also a director. And we had both done a few episodes on a TV series that now had a cult following so if we were known for anything it was that. But we weren't famous so we always thought why bother to tell anyone, it only confused people. However today was different and this is what happened.

In order to try and shorten what was going to be a long morning, Flavio said that since he had made up the contracts in both English and Italian for buyer and seller, though he was not representing the sellers, he knew that the translations were perfect and declared it would only be necessary for him to read it in Italian and that we could follow along in the English version. Marshall and I agreed, as usual. Anything to speed up the process I thought was a good idea.

Flavio began reading very rapidly and finally came to the section about 'occupation' which needed to be filled. I had expected him to simply tell the notary that we were retired writers but first he asked the sellers what their occupations were. I caught a note of sarcasm in his voice especially when he came to the Signora, who he obviously didn't like.

"And what are you?" he asked the husband, "It says here a seaman. Is that all you are? A seaman?"

The man looked perplexed but nodded.

Next he turned to her.

"And you. What are you?"

She narrowed her eyes slightly at him and then answered.

"A housewife."

"A what? Just a housewife?"

She nodded to the notary and gave him a very sweet smile.

"Very good. Seaman. And housewife," Flavio muttered scornfully and proceeded to fill in the spaces.

The notary then asked him, in Italian, what our occupations were and he sat bolt upright in his chair and exclaimed victoriously -

"She is a famous actress and he is a famous actor!"

Well, I just about dropped dead. The look on our seller's faces was one of complete surprise. We, of course, had told them nothing.

"Flavio," I whispered, "You were supposed to say that we were retired writers."

"I know, but when I heard your husband say he had worked with George Clooney I googled you."

After the contracts had been signed and witnessed by all we had to show the color of our money. Flavio opened a large leather briefcase. He produced the six drafts which we dutifully signed and then he removed the rest of the money, all in five hundred euro notes remember, and laid the one hundred and eighty thousand euros on the table and, just like a croupier in a Monte Carlo casino, pushed the six drafts and another one hundred and sixty thousand across the table toward the Signora and her husband in sixteen piles of ten thousand each. And, of course, all of it had to be counted!

The others, used to this ritual, stood up and stretched their legs. I had never seen anything like it but that wasn't all. As well as the minimal tax of 3% on the sixty thousand we had to pay about six thousand euros to the notary for his fee and other disbursements, another six thousand euros to the estate agent, she didn't even stay to count it but left immediately, and an equal amount to Flavio, all cash and, for them, tax-free! I just sat in my chair stunned. No wonder the Italian economy is having so much trouble.

Flavio approached the Signora and invited her to join us at the bar across the street to make a toast but, instead, she reached into her bag and took out a five euro bill, which is approximately seven dollars, and, declining the offer, gave it to him, saying -

"This is all I have. You see I have no money."

Flavio took the bill and came over to us and handed it to Marshall with a very sardonic smile.

"She would like to treat you to a *prosecco*. With this. Generous, no?"

That night back in our little villa we had our own celebration, good food, good wine, and then we hit our bed in relief.

But I was still very uneasy and had a strange dream. My body must have been trying to work out all the anxiety I had been feeling for almost two weeks. It was a ridiculous dream really.

I was washing the floor in our new house, in the corner of the rock room. I was dressed in a long bulky skirt and floral blouse. I wore no shoes. I was on my knees scrubbing and scrubbing the same spot on the floor.

Then I was no longer in the house but back in Flavio's inner office. It was almost an exact re-creation of what happened the day before except that in the dream everyone was dressed in 17th century costume. The notary had a large velvet hat and a thick chain from which hung a golden pendant with an emblem, a marking that looked exactly like one on the ceiling of the rock room that Elena had pointed out to us.

Flavio was equally flamboyantly dressed and so were all the others. They looked magnificent, as though they belonged in an oil painting by some famous Italian painter. There were bags of gold and precious objects spread all over the table. Even the Signora and her husband were extravagantly dressed. She was dripping with jewels and I noticed that everyone at the table wore the same chain and pendant, everyone except

Marshall and I. We were dressed just as we had been yesterday. There was a lot of talking but it wasn't in Italian, when suddenly Marshall stood and began desperately stuffing all the gold and jewels back into Flavio's briefcase. I tried to tell him to stop, that it wasn't ours anymore, but he kept on going. What would have happened next I don't know because Marshall was pushing and pulling at me to wake up.

"What? What's wrong?" I yelled.

"What's wrong with you?"

"What do you mean, I was dreaming."

"It must have been a nightmare, you were screaming in your sleep."

"You're crazy."

"It's not my sanity I'm worried about. What were you dreaming?"

"About the deal! Yesterday. All of us sitting there. Everyone was dressed in strange clothes and the table was covered in gold pieces."

I was sweating and Marshall wiped my forehead.

"Stressed out a little? It's over now. We've done it. No going back, my dear."

"I know. But it wasn't really that. It was something else I can't remember now. You shouldn't have woken me!"

"When your wife is screaming it's a good idea to wake her up."

"But now I've forgotten. Oh well, yes, I guess I have been stressed out. I thought I was dealing with the Borgias. You should have seen them all dressed up in marvelous costumes, ruff collars and big hats with feathers."

We laughed about it and talked through the whole event and how they did things differently here, their tradition and history, and soon we fell asleep again.

TWO

....

We didn't get into our house until a week after the possession date. The sellers kept buying time. Excuses like their new apartment wasn't ready, the water hadn't been connected, their new furniture hadn't arrived, they hadn't been able to unpack. The pleas only ran out when Flavio stepped in and said that was enough, they had to vacate the property of all their personal belongings by eight the next morning.

We spent our last night at the villa, having had to pay an extra week's lodging due to the inconvenience, feeling happy and finally relaxed about our new life as residents of the little town of Montevecchio.

We arrived with suitcases in tow and parked just below our new home in front of the tiny garage door, or we tried to. There was another car in our space so we had to park in a difficult and leaning sideways position on the street. I took the key from Marshall and hurried up the lane. I was so excited about being in the house again but just as I was putting the key into the lock the little white-haired woman poked her head out of her door and watched me. I knew it would be rude to ignore her so I turned and said with a smile

"Buongiorno!"

She smiled but immediately covered her mouth with her hand. She was unbelievably petite, four foot ten at the most, and as I looked her up and down I noticed she had on the cutest little black pumps that made her feet look even tinier than they were. How did she manage, at her age, on these cobblestones? I smiled again and then turned away from her to open the door.

Leaving it ajar, I went back to help Marshall with the luggage. The laneway was very steep and we were huffing and puffing a little coming up when the old woman came toward us offering to help. She was over eighty for God's sake, almost twice my age!

"No, *grazie*," we replied kindly.

She then went on to tell us not to leave the door open. I caught the word *'aperto'* which I understood but I noticed that she had a much thicker accent than the other Italians I had talked to. She mimed opening and closing the door firmly. We couldn't imagine what there was to worry about in such a small village but we thanked her and went inside.

I couldn't wait to get into the stone room and see it again. I immediately flung open the high arching doors and to my surprise a little old man was sitting on the step. He was startled and got up and I apologized for frightening him but the old woman came and admonished him for sitting there. It was obvious he was her husband. It was probably his favorite spot because the sun was warmest there and I felt he did have squatter's rights because he must have used that step for the past fifty years. I tried to tell the old woman that it was okay, that I didn't mind, but she shook her head and led him away.

We took our bags upstairs to the bedroom and went through the whole house making sure everything was in order and when we came back down to the stone room I noticed that a lovely handmade table was missing and had been replaced by a store-bought one.

"Oh well, maybe they decided to take it with them," Marshall said, "At least they replaced it."

"I know, but we paid for it and this one isn't as lovely."

Marshall was hoping I wouldn't start nitpicking and saying, 'They should have done this or should have done that' . . one of my most annoying qualities.

Everything in the kitchen seemed fine. The Signora had left dishes, cutlery and some old pots and pans. Unfortunately the oven didn't function and there was still quite a lot of junk for us to dispose of but that was all part of house buying.

The windows and shutters had been closed and as we went through the house we opened them all up. It was a beautiful day. The living room was much as I had remembered. Basically everything in the house was just as I had first seen it except the attic. It hadn't been cleaned out as Flavio had demanded and was filled with boxes of old blankets, old broken stereos, books and other odds and ends but really I finally didn't care a bit. The house was so inviting and I just wanted to get on with making it our own.

As I looked out over the balcony, I could see the square and the bar busy with the local trade, the wonderful smells from the bakery were as strong as ever and it was a clear day and the mountains were in full view.

We unpacked our few belongings and then we had to do some grocery shopping as there was nothing in the house. This meant, of course, trying to use our limited Italian but Marshall said we must be bold, so off we went.

We went to the butcher, the baker and the green grocer and did a lot of pointing. Afterwards we went to the little supermarket to stock up on the essentials, wine, oil etc. I was glad we had gone out right away because I had forgotten the shops closed on the dot of one and stayed closed till four in the afternoon.

I prepared lunch, typically Italian, I was a good cook then, and in the afternoon we decided to go out for a walk to the other side of the village that we hadn't explored before. As I said everything was shut, even the shutters on the houses. Everyone was clearly having their *siesta* but there were a few walkers who greeted us as the new owners of the house.

'*Bellissima,*' they kept saying. I wasn't sure if they meant the house or the weather but we returned their smiles and greetings.

When we got back the old woman was again watching us out of her window. I was getting a bit bothered by this constant peering. It seemed more than just a little nosy and I mentioned to Marshall that 'maybe we should have bought in the countryside' but he pooh-poohed me and said I was being paranoid and that to remember it was a small village and what else did the neighbors have to do.

We spent the next days doing much the same. Taking joy in simply walking and grocery shopping. The Italian products were always fresh and delicious. I tried different recipes, only Italian mind you because they didn't sell any international foods or spices. There was no such thing as curry and I couldn't for the life of me find oatmeal but who cared, I didn't want anything else but olives, cheese and sausage.

On our first Friday morning I was awakened by something more than the usual village sounds. I looked at the clock and it was only half past six. I went to open the shutters and the town was filled with food trucks and stalls and the vendors were busily laying out their wares. It was market day in Montevecchio. The locals were already there waiting to buy and chattering with each other.

"Now we know. Friday is market day. Look, Marshall!"

He came to the window and I pointed down to one truck that was all sausage and cheese and olives.

"And look, there's the little old lady. She's walking arm in arm with her husband."

We had our coffee at the café in the square. Then we meandered through the stalls buying this and that. As well as cheese there were shoes, vegetables, hardware, dresses, carpets, underwear, roast *porchetta* for sandwiches and we even came upon a fresh fish stand. And the fish were fresh, their eyes bulging and very alive. The man touched the clams to prove how fresh they were and they sputtered out water everywhere.

Although we lived not far from the ocean in America and you would have thought I could get fresh fish any time of the year, it wasn't so. They spray the fish with ammonia, so that you can't tell if it isn't fresh, but here in Montevecchio the fish was wonderful. I made *pasta con vongole*, bisques and one of my favorites was orati, an ocean perch that was just delicious, fried plain in a little butter with a pinch of salt. Oh, we ate well.

It got to the point where I had learned the words for most of what I wanted and now had decided it was time to invite some friends to our house, well, friends was optimistic, to invite our only friend, our lawyer Flavio, to dinner, in appreciation for all he had done for us.

In the meantime we had to get the shower fixed. The morning after we first arrived Marshall wanted to take a shower. He got in and pretty soon the stall was overflowing. The drain was clogged and the water went everywhere. So we needed to find a plumber. That was not an easy task. We didn't know anyone so Marshall asked the bar owner's daughter who spoke a little English if there was someone in town who could fix it. Eventually she found us an old fellow who was retired but said he would try and come that day.

I was sitting in the stone room, having coffee and learning my Italian, when the doorbell rang. I was still very shy about using my rudimentary vocabulary so I called Marshall down, chicken that I was. He answered the door and did his best to explain to the old man what he wanted done but even he was getting nowhere so he decided it was better to just take him upstairs and show him.

As I was sitting there, I suddenly noticed a pool of water in the corner of the room. I decided that maybe it was condensation from the dehumidifier and mopped it up and continued studying but before long another pool of water appeared. I knelt down and saw a small crack in the tile where the water was seeping through. Oh dear, another problem.

When Marshall and the plumbing man came down I showed them and the old man scratched his head for a moment, then said he thought he could fix it but would have to break open the tile. He also didn't know if he could return tomorrow or not. Things happened slowly in these little villages.

"Did he fix the shower?" I asked when he had gone.

"Not completely."

"What do I do about this?"

"Just keep mopping it up, I guess, till he can get to it."

He did return the next day and he brought a young lad with him. Before the old man went upstairs he showed his assistant to the stone room. The young man got his tools and broke up the tile. It didn't take him long. He showed me the leaky pipe and it took him no time to re-plumb it. While he waited for the old man he had a good look around the room.

"Bella, bella camera. Era una cantina, vero?"

I actually understood what he was saying and proudly replied, *"Si, una cantina."*

Finally Marshall and the old man came downstairs. He paid them and they left.

"Well, everything's fixed but we'll have to call someone to retile. It's only a little area. I think there are some of the same old tiles in the garage. I can probably do it."

I looked at him, not fully convinced of this. He wasn't much good with hammer and nail. But isn't that what men were supposed to do when they retired? Putter about fixing things?

He found the tiles but needed grout. He would stop at the hardware store on the way to the bank.

"You keep studying."

No easy task at my age so when he left I put the book down and, happy for any diversion, went over to the corner just to make sure that the pipe was definitely not leaking. I couldn't see much so I grabbed the flashlight from the kitchen and knelt down and peered into the hole.

Yes, the pipe was dry but something caught my eye, something shiny, copper-like. I reached in and, as I did, I cut myself. I carefully put my hand in a little farther and felt a sharp piece of metal. It wouldn't come loose but I pulled harder until it came free.

It was a metal box covered in dirt and sand. I rubbed it with my shirt. It was made of copper, darkened with moisture and aging. I took the box into the kitchen where I found some copper-cleaner. It cleaned up very well and revealed some detailed engraving. I tried to open it but the hinge was stuck and, though I pulled on it as carefully as I could, the lid broke off.

'Damn,' I thought, 'Now I've ruined it! I bet it was an antique.'

The box was not empty. There were papers, partly burnt, and ash at the bottom. I removed one of the pieces of paper. It had writing on it but I couldn't recognize the language.

It was a beautiful box and I was so sorry I had broken it. Maybe it could be mended. The town, after all, was famous for its copper-makers. I put it on the table in front of me and went back to trying to make head or tail of my Italian grammar. But I kept staring at the box and wondering where did it come from? Who had it belonged to? How old was it?

Marshall returned and came into the room.

"So are you being brilliant?"

"Don't be funny."

"What's that?"

He reached to pick up the box.

"Oh, be careful! Sorry, it's just that I've already damaged it trying to open it. The hinge broke."

"Where did you find it?"

"In there, in the hole, it was hidden under the tiles, and look," I said, pointing to the designs on the box,

"They're identical to those markings on the ceiling."

"Looks as though it's been there for a long time."

"I know. It's very old, and now I've ruined it."

"It's just a box. A pretty one at that."

"But look inside." I carefully opened the top. "See? All these burnt pieces of paper?" I lifted one of them out to show Marshall. "And look at the writing, is it Latin or what?"

He took the bit of paper and stared at it.

"I have no idea. My Latin is a little rusty. Well, I better get to those tiles. Oh, by the way, I met Flavio at the bank and invited him for dinner like we talked about, is that okay? He said Friday was best for him."

I was still concentrating on the piece of paper.

"What? Oh. Yes, sure, fine. Do you need help?"

Marshall smiled sardonically.

"Don't think I can do it, eh?"

"Of course you can. You're a master tiler, aren't you?"

"Don't let your imagination run away with you," he said, handing me the box, "It isn't the Holy Grail, you know. Probably not even worth much."

Friday came quicker than I expected. I wanted to cook up a real Italian dinner for Flavio but I was so nervous. I spent most of the morning trying to choose a menu. The Italians are fabulous cooks and I wanted to make it a very special evening. I decided on rabbit and ravioli. I was glad it was market day because I could get some fresh fish and make some of my bouillabaisse as a starter.

While I was practicing my culinary talents Flavio called to say that something had come up unexpectedly.

'Oh, no! He can't make it for dinner!'

Not at all. He was looking forward to dinner but he had just found out that on that very evening a professor of linguistics was going to hold a lecture in our village. Flavio was very interested in the history of the area and, specifically, the local dialects. He thought it might be very interesting for us to learn more about the town and its people. I told him it was a great idea. I didn't need to worry that it would interfere with our dinner because the lecture wasn't to start until nine. Nothing ever interferes with the Italians' love of eating.

So as I was preparing roasted rabbit and homemade ravioli, which took longer than I expected, there was a ring on the doorbell. It was Flavio and Marshall led him into the kitchen.

"Ciao, Flavio!" I said, giving him a kiss.

"Mmm, something smells good!"

"I hope it will be. I'm cooking Italian tonight. Well, I cook Italian every night but it will be 'special Italian' tonight. I hope you'll like it."

He handed me two bottles of wine and a large blue

cardboard box.

"What is that?" I asked, wiping the flour off my hands.

"It is a cake. A mimosa."

"Lovely name for a cake. You know, I never make dessert. Can't it seems, have the wrong energy, nothing works out. So, thank you. You've saved me!"

"I think you will like this. But it must be in the cool."

"Is the refrigerator okay?"

"Yes, very good."

"Marshall, why don't you show him the house while I get this all on the go. It won't take long."

When I was ready to serve the soup they were already in the stone room drinking wine and nibbling on the cheese, boar's sausage and olives that I had set out for them. As I laid the tureen on the table Flavio exclaimed to me rather joyously-

"This is a very beautiful house. It is so unexpected. When I met that woman I had no idea she had such good taste. This room is remarkable."

We had a wonderful evening. The meal was a success. Flavio commented especially on the rabbit.

"It is even better than how my mother cooks it."

After a brief pause for digestion I went to get the cake and coffee. I didn't know what to expect when I opened the box. Mimosa was the perfect word for such a cake. It was delicious looking. It was made of pale cream and bits of lemon cake molded together to make it look like a creamy cloud, all delicate and light.

We had two helpings each and it was gone.

"Oh, Flavio, thank you, that was so good!"

"We try," he said with a sly grin.

We didn't have much time left. I begged Marshall not to bother with the dishes. Being an Englishman he believes in cleaning up immediately after a meal. I cook, he washes.

"We can do it tomorrow. I don't want to miss this lecture."

We drank our coffee and were getting ready to go when I remembered the box and went back into the stone room to get it.

"What is that?" Flavio asked curiously.

"Oh, yes, look at it."

He took it.

"Please be careful. I already broke the hinges. You see, the top?"

"Where did you find this?"

"It was hidden beneath some tiles we had to take up when we were fixing a leaky pipe. But come, I want to show you something."

I took him back into the stone room.

"You see the tiles above that you admired earlier?"

"Yes."

"The designs are the same as on the box. And look inside."

I showed him the contents.

"Interesting. What are you going to do with it?"

"I thought maybe the professor might know something about it. So I thought I'd bring it along."

We left the house and started walking down towards the piazza and I felt again that I was being watched. I turned slightly and saw the old woman looking out the window.

As we entered the town hall I noticed that there were very few people in attendance. A small group were sitting together near the back. There were also some British ex-pats that I had met briefly at the market. The professor had set up an overhead projector and he had books and papers on the table. We followed Flavio and sat near the front.

The professor greeted us in Italian and English. He asked if anyone didn't understand Italian and only Marshall and I raised our hands but Flavio told the professor that he could continue in Italian, that he would translate for us if it wouldn't cause any disturbance.

"Yes, of course," the professor answered.

I was feeling ashamed of myself. If these people spoke my language it was about time I took my studying seriously. I took note, believe me.

Before the lecture started the professor handed out little pamphlets.

"This is a dictionary of words used only by the people of this *comune*. I thought it might be interesting to you all since that is the reason for this lecture and I am sure that some of you could add to the list."

I looked behind me as I could hear that a few people were already leaving. Flavio opened the pamphlet.

"I was given a booklet similar to this one," he said, "One day when I was in the third grade we were getting ready for an excursion to Montevecchio to visit the birthplace of a newly beatified, how do you say it, a sainted nun, Beata Maria della Palombara. You live on a street named after her and our teacher gave out these little books."

I opened the pamphlet. There were about two hundred words listed in it that were completely different from their familiar Italian counterpart.

"The reason for this was because, for as long as anyone can remember, the people of this town have been difficult for others to understand."

"But you only lived thirty kilometers away!"

"Yes, I know. And this is only the second time I have been to this village."

"Why?"

"I do not know. Maybe because we were always told that the people of this town were not really Italians."

The professor had stopped his lecture and seeing that there were only a handful of people left in the room, most of them *stranieri*, he decided to go on in English.

"It seems as though not many Italians are interested in this topic. I'm sure it must be a repetition for them since they know the dialect much better than we do. I thought they might want to add new information but I suppose not. So, if you would still like me to, I will continue."

"Oh, yes, definitely," I said.

"Yes? So, I will give you a brief history. The village of Montevecchio lies castled atop a hill six hundred meters above sea level. It was first conceived as a fortified shelter during the barbarian invasions that began during the 5th century. It became a thriving community and by the 14th century Montevecchio had a population of more than nine thousand. It has always been known as the village of coppersmiths. Many of these people had come from somewhere else, no one is sure, possibly Albania, Romania or Turkey. They brought with them the art of copper. Here you can see some examples."

He held up a book.

"They created everything from kitchenware to religious icons and tools to weapons, such as daggers and axes, and even cult objects like this one."

The picture was of an animal with wings holding a dagger in one hand and a spoon in the other.

"As you can see, the work was beautiful and only long experience could achieve it. Copper handicraft in Montevecchio is an ancient practice and its memory has been handed down through many centuries. Its origins are unknown because there are no records. Their presence was first recorded in the 14th century but now there are only a handful of such artisans left and the town has been reduced to five hundred inhabitants. What happened to all these people? Why did they leave? Other towns and villages in the area prospered and even increased in population yet almost eighty percent of the houses here were abandoned by the year 1920.

"The birthrate is what is most curious. In the rest of Italy it slumped very suddenly in the sixties and seventies but here it has always decreased little by little. I have gone through the church documents, what is left of them, and I have discovered that for some unknown reason the townspeople here have had a consistently and abnormally low fertility rate for many centuries.

"But I diverge from my primary thesis, to try and locate the origin of their dialect and the reasons for its continued existence in the modern world."

Flavio, always the lawyer ready with a question, put up his hand and asked -

"Professor, I am also very interested in the history of our area and have done a lot of reading and research myself, and lately have been trying to restore some of our heritage ruins, but I too have come across very little written about this town. I myself remember as a child being given a similar pamphlet to this one when our school came on the bus for a visit. This is only the second time in my life I have been here and that is due to my new American friends. I wonder if you are aware of the legend of Boro that surrounds the mystery of these so-called copper people?"

"Yes, I am and it is a very colorful legend. I will get to it shortly. To go back to the pamphlet though, it only contains a small selection because there are many, many more examples that I was hoping the locals could add to this list, but as I said, obviously they have no interest. These examples, such as ears which are called *"campane"* (bells), shoes *"fangose"* (muddy), wine *"frizzu"* (sparkling), chickens *"ruspanti"* (free-range), teeth *"mordenti"* (biting), a hat *"cimusu"* (top-piece), playing cards *"sfoiose"* (leafed through), were noted by Cesare Lombroso who studied this dialect and included them in his book, *Archivio di Psichiatria*, in 1899. He drew many diagrams describing these words. But what follows . . "

The professor turned to six unidentifiable objects on the next page.

" . . is of great interest. No one is sure what these patterns represent or what they really are. They are very simple symbols as you see here."

He pointed to one of them and I gasped!

"Flavio, look! The identical pattern that's on my box," I whispered.

"This is a very large copper plate," the professor went on, turning the page again, "Nearly a meter in diameter and it dates back to the 14th century and the engraving is directly related to the legend of Boro.

"It is a fanciful story but not very well known. According to Adolfo Leoni and Mario Fugazza, who collected legends of the territory, Boro was originally from Northern India and very skillful with metals and taught the art to the young people of the town. But another gypsy, a young thief, was jealous of Boro's ability and talent and continually taunted him, making him curse and swear in anger. It was a great sin to curse the Divine and the boy spread gossip around the town that Boro was mad and possessed by the Devil. And to realize this false prophecy the boy stole into Boro's house in the middle of the night and thrust an incandescent sphere into his mouth as he was sleeping and Boro's face became deformed and his voice hoarse and he could only communicate in foreign sounds. The local people feared him when they saw him and he was chased out of the town.

"Now, abandoned by everyone, Boro made his home in the mountains where he continued to produce wonderful copper, the most beautiful he had ever made. One of his most treasured pieces found its way back into the village. An alleged drawing of this piece was found many, many years ago. You see? It is a large engraving of a beautiful woman with a child in her arms. The woman is weeping, her head bent low over the child. And here, she is holding a dagger in one hand and a large spoon in the other. But who knows if these depictions Lombroso found are authentic.

"The townspeople came to believe that Boro's art was divine, not to mention very lucrative, and they went out in search of him but he had vanished never to be seen or heard from again. So they began to copy his work and his methods which have now been handed down from son to son. And the term used for the strange speech adopted by these craftsman is called *baccaiamento* which, loosely translated, means 'speaking aloud'."

I was completely enthralled by this whole story.

The lecture came to a close. The British contingent thanked the professor and left but we stayed behind. I needed to ask some questions and I desperately wanted to show the professor the box and, in particular, the designs which were so similar to the ones he had held up for us to see during his lecture.

Marshall and Flavio were looking through the booklet and Flavio was teaching him how to pronounce some of the Montevecchio words so I approached the professor. I put the box on the table. He noticed it immediately and stopped what he was doing.

"Where did you get this, Signora?"

"I found it in my house. Well, actually, I found it under some tile we had to remove because of a water problem."

He carefully lifted the box.

"Oh, please be careful, I've already broken it."

He studied the outside of the box and then lifted the cover carefully and looked inside. A strange expression had come over his face. I added quickly -

"The symbols are exactly the same design that is on my ceiling tiles."

"Where is this house?" he inquired.

"Only a few meters from here. Would you like to come up for a coffee or a drink?"

"Yes, I would. Very much."

"Marshall, the professor is coming to the house," I announced.

We waited while he finished packing up his belongings and went outside to where he had parked his car. It was dark but the bar next door to the town hall was jumping and the old men were playing cards. I was surprised that so many people were wandering about. Why hadn't they come to the lecture? I'm sure the professor must have been disheartened to see the square so full.

"It is surprising," he remarked quietly, as we stood taking in the warmth and the sounds of the night, "It is still a very poor town. No library, bookstore, not very much to aid the mind."

"Nothing except two enormous churches," Marshall added with a sly grin, "Two convents filled with nuns, a *palazzo* for the priests and a view so spectacular that my heart stops beating."

"You are a poet, Signor, but I agree, it has the most beautiful setting of anywhere I have been. It is as though time stood still here on this hilltop."

He pointed to the people at the bar and strolling in the square.

"They are all related, you know, like the roots of one tree."

As we approached our front door I saw the old woman again peering from behind the shutter. 'They should be asleep,' I thought. Did she know we went to the lecture? No doubt she did. The shutter quickly closed.

Inside the house Marshall took the professor into the stone room while Flavio and I got the coffee and some liqueurs ready. I put the box on the kitchen table.

"Flavio, do you know anything about those designs? Have you ever seen them before, like in one of those churches you restored. You must have seen them somewhere in all that history you read."

"No, I have not. But then we are an ancient civilization. There are thousands of symbols, pagan, Christian, Gnostic, Arabic, Greek, Etruscan, Jewish. Although Italians are religious, we are also a very superstitious race. Underneath our Catholicism thrives a healthy dose of paganism. Take my village for example. We too have a legend. It is the legend of Sibilla. The mountains you see out your window are named after her. In Italy, the mistress of this magic mountain was called 'wise Sibilla'. Her underworld paradise was entered through a grotto in the mountains of Norcia, a region famed for its witches. Nearby is a magical lake fed by water from a cavern. The mountain abounded in amorous pleasures. The goddess blessed those who visited and when they returned to the world they passed the rest of their days in joy. There is much chatter among the locals. One told me a story about a knight who came upon Sibilla on her mountain and enjoyed all the pleasures of music, love and feasting. The knight did not want to leave but feared he would be damned if he stayed. At last he pulled himself away and set off for Rome to get absolution from the pope. It was denied. The man's servant begged that they return to *'le montagne della Sibilla'* and they did. Later the pope changed his mind and sent messengers to look for them but they had disappeared. Sibilla is called 'the true mother of the Messiah' . . a female Messiah. There are many living in these mountains who believe in this legend and still follow and practice the arts of Sibilla."

"I can tell fortunes. My grandmother taught me."

"That is because you are Catholic and superstitious."

"No, I'm not. I'm an ex-Catholic."

"There is no such thing as an ex-Catholic."

"Oh Flavio, that's just semantics. You know I don't believe in God."

"That has very little to do with it. There is no exit, *carina*."

"Oh, all right, I know what you're trying to say but the coffee is getting cold."

We brought the coffee into the stone room and saw Marshall holding a ladder and the professor was perched at the top of it with a flashlight in his hand, peering closely at the designs on the ceiling.

"Very interesting. And you say you found the box there below those tiles?"

"Yes, it happened by accident. I never would have found it if the pipe hadn't burst."

"May I see it again?"

I went back to the kitchen for the box and returned and handed it to the professor. He opened it carefully and took out a few fragments of the burnt paper.

"Do you recognize any of the letters or words?" I asked.

"Yes, some words but there are some letters which are of a different alphabet. Would you mind if I took the box to my city? There is a man who has studied many languages and is a scholar of the east. I would like him to see this. Maybe he will be able to help us."

We drank our coffee and, as it was getting very late, the professor had to leave.

"I have a long drive back to Rome where I am visiting with family."

"You are welcome to stay here for the night. It's almost three hours drive to Rome."

"I am used to it. But it has been a very fascinating evening for me. I didn't expect these circumstances. I was just hoping for more details for my book but I have received much more than I had anticipated. As soon as I have any information I will phone you."

I went for his coat.

"Marshall, did you give the professor our number?"

"Yes, he did."

"Please don't lose the box."

"Do not be concerned. I will take great care of it. Thank you for a wonderful evening. You will be hearing from me soon. And please call me Luigi."

Flavio thanked him also and they spoke in Italian, then he shook his hand and Marshall said he would walk the professor to his car.

"Well, I must say things are getting very interesting," Flavio said with a smile after they had gone, "When I said you were superstitious, I was right. Only superstitious people have strange things happening to them."

"Oh Flavio, it was all just coincidence."

"Are you sure?"

I looked at him quizzically and shuddered, as though a ghost walked up my spine.

"Please, now you're making me feel strange."

He laughed.

"I am sorry. Don't worry, this house has wonderful vibrations. It is very inviting and I am sure that there are only good ghosts haunting it. The box is just that. A box that someone used to hold their documents or something precious. You know, I have the feeling that you belong here. Somehow Montevecchio suits you in my mind. Or you suit it. Next I will make a dinner for you to meet my friends. *Ciao e grazie* for the wonderful company and food. It was one of the best evenings I have had in a long time. I think now I will thank the Signora for all her trouble and her manipulations because it was she who brought you two here to this town. Interesting. *Ciao, ciao.*"

"Don't forget the *festa* on Friday."

We kissed on the cheeks and he left.

Closing the door, I turned to Marshall and said -

"Well, what do you think?"

"I could live out the rest of my days here. And you could bury me here or throw my ashes into the Adriatic."

"Oh Marshall, you always talk of death when something wonderful happens. Oh, my goodness, I totally forgot. Michael is coming tomorrow!"

"Yup, I'm picking him up at the airport around one o'clock. We should be back in Montevecchio by four."

"I wonder what he'll make of our little village?"

We left the dirty dishes and went to bed with the shutters open. An accordion was playing in the distance and I slept peacefully and didn't remember a dream or a nightmare.

THREE

....

Early the next morning, as Marshall left for the airport, the town was already hopping. Men were putting up lights all along the streets and women were dressing up every doorway with flower arrangements for a festival, or *sagra*, to celebrate the summer solstice that apparently was unique to Montevecchio.

I had all day to buy our groceries and make up Michael's room and get dinner ready. The weather was lovely and there was no chance of rain in the forecast. I knew that Michael would love the drive up and that Marshall would show him some of the local sights on the way.

While I was making the beds the doorbell rang. I didn't want to run all the way down the stairs so I opened the shutters and there was the old woman holding a beautifully wrapped gift in her hand. I asked her to wait a moment and went down to open the door.

She looked even smaller than I remembered but she did have the most beautiful snowy white hair that wound ever so perfectly around her tiny head. She handed me the gift and said a few words like *'un piccolo regalo'* that I understood, that this was a present for the *'sagra'* and to accept it.

I thanked her and apologized for not speaking Italian. She smiled and again her hand went up to her mouth but this time I noticed why she did it. Her teeth were totally black. It stunned me a little. She said something about 'coffee' and pointed to her door. I answered as best I could, saying that I was expecting visitors and maybe another time. We shook hands and she went back across the road and turned with a little wave as she disappeared into her house.

I closed the door gently and went to the kitchen to open the package. It was a box of chocolates and a bottle of local brandy. What a lovely thought! I must do something for her. I'd think about that later.

It was almost five in the afternoon when they arrived.

"Hello, darling!"

Michael came bursting in with his usual large array of bags.

"I thought you were just staying for the weekend," I teased.

"Oh, yes darling, of course, but you know me. I have my video camera and vitamins and biscuits and teas, the usual. My God, the drive was spectacular. And the sun, the heat! Just what I needed."

"Well, get yourself settled. Dinner is on the go and we can sit and have drinks."

"Good-o! Show me the way, old man."

Marshall led him upstairs and I could hear him 'oohing' and 'aahing' about the house and the views as they made their way up to the top floor.

I was now becoming obsessed with Italian food. I actually made my own pasta for the shrimp lasagna, shrimp was Michael's favorite dish and lasagna was his second. It wasn't nearly as difficult as I thought it would be. I had created a platter of the best Italian antipasto that I could find and I had everything arranged in my beautiful rock room by the time Marshall and Michael came downstairs.

"This house is fantastic. You still always surprise me, you two! Of all the beautiful places you've lived in how the hell did you find this one? And this?"

He walked around the room.

"What is this? It looks like a bloody crypt."

"It is actually and we found the house on the internet."

"Naw, come on!"

"It's true! Just believe me when I tell you that it's probably been the most unusual experience we've ever had."

"You must tell me about it."

"Oh, it's a long story."

I looked at Marshall and we both smiled.

"How was the flight?"

"Just awful. I hate flying. Puts me in cold sweats and terror."

"But it's only two hours, isn't it?"

"Much worse! Don't have time to get used to it at all, just up and then down!"

I went to the table and poured us some wine.

"How's your sister?" I asked, handing Michael his glass.

"Wonderful. Working, trying to save lives, writing pamphlets on the health and welfare that's non-existent in our well-developed nation."

"So what would you like to do this weekend, since you only have three days?" asked Marshall.

"Whatever's on the cards, old man. Take me anywhere."

"You know the festival starts officially tomorrow. We have no idea what to expect. So we'll all have to play it by ear."

"Fine with me."

Michael was still wandering about and taking in the room.

"Remarkable. Must be as old as, well, as . . "

"The 14th century," I interrupted.

"What are those designs all about?"

He was pointing to the tiles on the ceiling.

"We don't really know," Marshall said, pouring him another

drink, "But they're some kind of symbols dating back hundreds of years."

"What, you mean they're original?"

"That's what the owners said but who knows really." I offered him some antipasto. "Taste that sausage, it's delicious."

"And who were these people you bought the house from?"

"Well, he worked on a fishing boat that sailed to Africa. He was a technician, we think, and she was a housewife, except that we did find out this room was once her restaurant, but it closed after two years, don't know why. They were just locals. They'd lived here all their lives."

"Fantastic. And why did they sell it?"

"Marshall, you tell him the story. I'll go check on dinner."

"What are we having? Something Italian I hope?"

"Lasagna. Shrimp lasagna."

"A woman after me own heart!"

I hurried into the kitchen. I didn't want to find everything burnt.

The kitchen window was open and I heard chanting and voices and, as I looked out, I saw many people making their way past the house down to the square. It was getting dark and the procession was just below. I went to the front door and opened it. The laneway was filled with people chanting something that seemed familiar to my ear. A psalm or prayer, I was sure of that. Michael and Marshall had heard them also and were already standing behind me.

"Let's go upstairs. We'll get a better view from the balcony."

Once up in the den, we opened the French doors and could see three or four hundred people following four men carrying a pallet with a statue of the Virgin Mary, festooned with wildflowers and holding a basket of fresh strawberries.

"Oh, God, where's my camera! Wonderful, wonderful! Can dinner wait? I'd love to get some pictures out there."

"I guess it can. You and Marshall go ahead, I'll keep it warm."

They dashed out the front door and I could see them through the kitchen window as they hurried to catch up.

I got myself another glass of wine and sat by the window. The night was picturesque. I turned the lights off in the kitchen. The town was lit up like a Christmas tree and you could see all the villages in the surrounding hills.

It was peaceful sitting there in the semi-darkness but it was interrupted by a scratching noise. Oh God, I hoped we didn't have rats. I went to the hallway to listen and then into the stone room. The noise was stronger there and I heard voices. Maybe people next door were saying their prayers but it sounded as though it was coming from below the floor. I must be crazy, I thought. I went back into the kitchen and waited for Marshall and Michael. What was taking them so long? I checked the lasagna and it was starting to dry out so I turned off the oven and went out looking for them.

Of course, I found them in the bar.

"Well, here you are you two. You know dinner is beyond ready."

"Oh sorry, darling. Michael wanted a quick aperitif."

"Strange people these Italians. All this superstitious stuff. Praying, spouting mumbo-jumbo. The Brits would be appalled. Well, let's get back and eat, I'm starving!"

We returned to the house. As I walked in the door I listened for any sounds. I went into the stone room. Nothing. It must have been my imagination.

After dinner, I left the two best friends to chat on their own and went to bed with, what else, my Italian study book. I could hear music and a gentle hubbub of sound. I opened the shutters and looked out and, as usual, the bar and the square were still full of strolling people and old men playing cards. What Michael said was true. They were superstitious and deeply entrenched in the rituals of the Catholic Church but I felt that there was something rather beautiful in all the ceremony and tradition. How good it must feel not to have to question existence and death.

I lay down again and tried conjugating some simple verbs and I must have fallen asleep because I don't remember anything else till the next morning. Marshall was dead to the world. They must have stayed up very late because Marshall rarely sleeps in.

I got dressed and took my study book with me downstairs and made myself a cup of coffee and the doorbell rang. I hoped it wasn't the old lady again. I went to the door and opened it and there was a handsome young boy with a fresh bouquet of flowers. He asked me if it was all right to attach it to the corner of the house and I nodded, 'of course'.

The doorbell must have woken Marshall up because he came downstairs in his shorts and T-shirt looking the worse for wear.

"Any coffee?" he asked huskily.

"Sure, I just made some. You two stay up late?"

"Yeah, too late. We went up to the historical square. Michael wanted to take a look at it but it was too dark to shoot video. We met the man who owns the bar. His name is Angelo and he made us some strange concoctions. I think he put absinthe in them. We had no idea what we were saying. All gobble-de-gook Italian, I'm sure."

"What time did you get in?"

"God knows."

I handed him his espresso.

"What time do the bars stay open?"

"As long as they want, I think."

"You look like you need some eggs and bacon."

"Good idea. I'll go wake him up. But I'll jump in the shower first."

I started getting breakfast ready and Michael came into the kitchen. He looked worse than Marshall.

"Got anything to drink?"

"How about a little absinthe?"

"Oh God, is that what we drank last night?"

"Marshall thinks so."

"No, no, darling, water, juice, or even better a cup of tea. Wait. I'll bring it down."

"No, no, I have some English tea here. Want some bacon and eggs?"

"Love some, darling, but tea first, if you don't mind."

"So you met Angelo?"

"What a character! Haven't a clue what he said, or what your husband said to him, but really a character. A little shifty, I thought. God, booze is cheap here."

I made him his cup of tea.

"Oh, thank you darling. Tell me, why is that historical square all empty? Most of it is boarded up, nothing there except the bar and the bloody church."

"I don't know. They say the town has fallen on hard times for years and years. No money for restoration, I guess, like in the other villages."

"Shame really. It could be quite spectacular."

"The estate girl told us that no one buys in this *comune* except in the countryside. She told me that no self-respecting Italian would buy here but I don't know why. It's so beautiful."

"Well, it is unique. Last night Marshall drove me around a bit before we went to the bar. He took me to a point on the road where you could view the whole town perched on the top of its dark hill. Eerie."

"The town? But that's only because it's so old and in disrepair."

"I thought it looked like the village of Dracula!"

"Oh Michael, you're being dramatic. It's just an old town."

Marshall came down looking much more like himself. I served out the bacon and eggs.

"Feeling better?" I said laughingly.

"Much," Marshall answered.

"Speak for yourself, old man. What on earth did we drink last night?"

"The devil's brew!"

"What are you two going to do today?"

"Why? What are you up to?" Marshall asked.

"I thought you'd be taking Michael out sight-seeing."

"We could do that."

"I'd love a good walk. Is there anywhere to take a good walk?"

"The whole countryside is at your disposal."

"Good, I'll shower and shave and then you can lead me on. What about you, darling?"

"Oh, I've got things to do, don't worry about me. I'm not an avid hiker like you and Marshall."

"Doctor said I must. Need the exercise. I went for a check-up and there seems to be a little bit of heart trouble."

"Oh?"

"Nothing serious, nothing that walking, no fried foods and less alcohol couldn't cure!"

"Well, off you both go. Don't bother about the dishes,

Marshall. We have a dishwasher and I'd like to check it out."

"I hate dishwashers, more trouble than they're worth," he muttered.

"I'll just do my ablutions and be with you in a flash."

Michael went upstairs.

"Do you think it's serious?" I asked Marshall.

"You mean his heart? No, he's as strong as a horse. Always has been. He's just a bit of a hypochondriac."

"Oh. Good."

"We won't be long. I'll just take him down the road past the corner there and into the countryside. It's not a bad walk, not too steep."

"All right, but remember that Flavio is coming to the festival tonight to see the man on stilts or clown or whatever he is."

"Oh yes, I forgot."

"I'll make you some sandwiches and you better take plenty to drink."

After the boys left I took a walk to the square below the house. They were setting up a bandstand and the whole town was busy preparing for the festivities and I was stopped by a middle-aged woman.

"Excuse me. You are English, aren't you?"

She certainly was.

"Yes, well, I'm American."

"I was wondering, is that your house above the square?"

"Yes."

"I'm told it's very beautiful."

"Yes, it is, I suppose."

"An Italian friend of mine lived in that house many, many years ago and she wanted me to ask you if she could see it again."

I was a bit taken aback. I wasn't sure I wanted to show it to just anyone.

"Well . . "

"She's waiting at the bar. Come, I'll introduce you. Oh, and my name is Martha."

As we reached the bar an extremely pretty, middle-aged woman with a very gentle face got up and came to greet us. She didn't speak any English so Martha translated.

"Yes, I suppose she can see the house. When would she like to?"

She asked the woman and her face lit up into a broad smile. *"Quando sarebbe comodo per la Signora."*

"She says whenever it's convenient for you."

"Well, we have company at the moment. Sometime after the festival, maybe next week?"

We set a time for next Wednesday after lunch.

I walked away thinking that Italians had a remarkable talent for insinuating themselves without at all being offensive. Somehow it's difficult to refuse them. I hoped Marshall wasn't going to fuss about it.

When I got to the house the boys still hadn't returned and, although I should have gone back to studying, I decided to take a walk up the laneway into the old historical central square. It was going to be the main location for the *festa* and I was curious to see what was going on.

As I walked I noticed the houses. It was true that a lot of the buildings were empty and boarded up but all along there was activity. The decorations were everywhere and people were setting up little market stalls in the cantinas. They were really just cold rooms on the floor below their apartments and either used as a shop in the old days or more likely now as storage and to keep wine and cheeses and sausage. I passed one where a shoemaker was working. It was a tiny space with no windows and the lane was so narrow that sunlight could only rarely reach it but he seemed very content at what he was doing and didn't even look up at me when I stopped to watch him.

Then I heard a constant tapping further on and followed the sound.

It led me into another tiny lane. There was more to the village than I thought. I followed the tapping down some steps, along another even narrower lane and stopped at the end of a passage where a short stocky white-haired man was leaning over an enormous urn. He had a small hammer and a round piece of metal and he tapped the urn continually.

So here, at last, was a coppersmith.

He greeted me very warmly and asked if I wanted to see inside his shop. It was filled to the rafters with hundreds of copper objects. There were bowls of every size, urns, utensils and beautiful plates with designs of the Madonna, animals, fruits and birds. I had never in my life seen so much copper. He showed me everything hoping, of course, for a sale but when I asked him the price of some of the pieces I just about fell over. Most of them were over five hundred, some even thousands of euros. I told him they were beautiful but that I would have to bring my husband.

He explained to me that his father and grandfather had all been coppersmiths but now he was the only one left and his sons weren't interested. He said that they used to take the copper in wagons down the mountain to the markets all over this part of Italy. He wanted to talk so I let him but I only got the bare gist of what he was saying. I thanked him and we shook hands and he went back to his work.

I reached the square and saw more tables being set up. The

bar was crowded. It was a very tiny place. I poked my head in but thought, no, I wasn't quite ready, so I continued on towards the church.

There were actually two churches in the town, one almost directly below the other. The smallest, on the opposite side of the square from the bar, was the oldest of the two and I went in. It was beautiful. Flowers were everywhere. The altar was very simple and the pews were worn smooth with age. I walked around looking at the little side chapels dedicated to different saints. Here the predominant saint was the nun who had been recently beatified, Santa Maria della Palombara.

Most of the church was inviting and open but one of the chapels was completely enclosed by an ornate copper grating. I went to open the door in the grating but it was locked. Inside the alcove was an altar and underneath the altar sat a glass box and in it was a mummified body dressed in the white habit of a nun. It must have been Beata Maria. On the wall above hung a huge crucifix with the usual tortured body of Christ but the design of the copper grating was what interested me the most. It was exquisite and, as I studied it more closely, maybe it was my imagination but I could see, I am sure they were, the same symbols that were on my ceiling. The curves and spirals and squares were exactly the same. How old was it? And who created it? The old coppersmith I had met? I thought maybe I'll ask him and then remembered that the boys should be back by now and, after lingering for a few more moments, returned home.

They were standing by the stone balustrade across the laneway from our front door chatting and looking down toward the green fields in the valley below. Marshall was pointing out something in the near distance, probably the road they had traveled.

"Well, you two must have walked all the way to the next village."

"We did actually. Must have gone about ten miles. Where have you been?"

"Just up in the square. I visited the little church. There's a body in there."

"What body?" asked Michael.

"I think it must be the remains of the nun, Sister Beata. She's been mummified."

"Good for her," Marshall replied with indifference. Catholicism and its superstitious beliefs were anathema to him. We rarely discussed religion.

"Oooh, I'd love to get some footage of that! I'm going to take a shower. My God, the women are scrumptious here!" Michael exclaimed as he went inside.

"You better watch out for him," I warned Marshall, "This is a Catholic village and you know these people."

"Oh, it's mostly talk. But you're right, he is an old goat. I think they'll see him coming a mile away. Anyway, he's got his camera and he'll be too busy filming everything, or should I say the video of the 'Life and Exploits of Michael Hunt'?"

"He never turns that camera off. Does he go home and just watch it all?"

"No, he edits it. All of it. He has hundreds of tapes, all to do with his life."

"Well, he doesn't have any kids and he isn't married. Who is he saving it for?"

"Posterity, darling. We all need to leave something for posterity."

"Well, please tell him not to film me anymore, I'm tired of seeing myself age in his videos."

"But look at that beautiful face I love so much."

"Oh stop. Go on, get ready."

Marshall gave me a soft kiss.

"You are beautiful you know, you just don't see what I see."

Once inside the house we could hear Michael singing his heart out in the shower. What else, *O sole mio, à la* Dean Martin. The only problem was that Michael was tone-deaf.

FOUR

....

Marshall and Michael had already left. Michael was desperate to start his filming before dusk. I poured myself a glass of wine and was sitting in the stone room. I had opened the cathedral doors so I could watch the people passing by. Suddenly a head popped in and it startled me a little.

"Flavio! I didn't expect you so soon."

"What do you mean? I said eight and it is eight," he said matter-of-factly as he came in and handed me two bottles of what I knew would be superb wine.

"Thank you. Would you like some?"

"Yes, please. Where is Marshall?"

"Oh, he went ahead with our friend Michael from London who's staying with us for a few days. Michael couldn't wait to start filming everything that's going on at the *festa*."

I opened the bottle, poured him a glass and replenished mine.

"I am sorry to tell you but I can only stay an hour. I must return to have dinner with my mother."

"Well then, we better go find Marshall. I hope you won't miss seeing the man on the stilts. But I'm sure Michael will get it all on tape."

We left via the cathedral doors and again Flavio commented on their beauty.

"Yes, I only wish they didn't look straight at the old lady's house across the way. Her husband sits on this stoop every morning to get the sun. I don't open the door if he's there so

I won't disturb him."

"You are always so careful. It is very kind, I know, but you must not feel badly. This is your house now."

"But he's probably been sitting on this stoop for the past forty years. I feel he has squatter's rights."

He laughed and we walked arm in arm with our wine up to the central square.

Our entire passage was lit with candles set in small bags of sand. There were narrow tables all along the walls of the laneway which was closed to traffic because of the festival. People were selling jewelry, icons and food and at the entrance to the piazza a group of musicians were playing and singing.

As we entered the square I thought I'd never be able to find Marshall because there were already hundreds of people milling about. Normally the square was eerily empty except in the evening when the locals frequented the small bar. People in historical costumes were cooking Italian foodstuffs on small barbeques. There were lines at every food stall.

I couldn't see Marshall anywhere.

"Let's look in the bar."

It was practically impossible to get in. We pushed our way through and at the end of the bar we could see Michael and Marshall talking to some people I didn't recognize and Angelo, the barman. Michael, of course, was filming.

We managed to get over to them and Marshall greeted Flavio and then introduced us to his newfound friends. Luckily enough some of them spoke a little English and anyway I had my trusted bilingual lawyer at my side. Everyone introduced themselves.

"This is Marten, he's from Holland and he is married to this lady, who is French but now lives near Montevecchio."

"Buona sera. This is Flavio, a friend of mine," I said.

"Sera a tutti," he offered, shaking everyone's hand.

"Marshall, Flavio can only stay for an hour so maybe we should take him around the town. We can come back later."

Marshall turned to Michael who was filming us and said -

"Michael, put that damn thing down and meet our wonderful friend, Flavio. What are you drinking?"

Marshall was looking a little pink-cheeked and doe-eyed. Michael lowered the camera and patted Flavio on the shoulder.

"How are you? I hope you speak English. I'm as lost as a lamb!"

"Yes, good evening."

"What are we drinking? This wonderful man, Angelo, the man! He's made up some special potion."

Marshall raised his glass for a toast. I looked at their glasses. The liquid in them was a translucent aqua green.

Flavio whispered to me -

"It is absinthe."

"That's illegal at home."

"It's a love potion," Michael assured me, "Try it."

I took a sip. It went down smooth and warm. 'Better stay clear of this,' I thought.

"Meet Angelo. He's incredible."

I shook the barman's hand.

"Sera," I said and then turned to Marshall, "I think we better get some food before you drink another drop of this 'love potion'!"

We pushed our way back outside

"Let's go over there, the line looks shorter," Michael suggested and strode off.

"Fegato. What is that?" he asked as we got to the stall.

"Liver," I said.

He turned a little green but there was a beautiful girl standing there waiting to serve us. She must have been one of the tallest people in the village. She had long black hair and dark eyes and beautiful pale skin. I had seen her many times in the café below our house. Michael decided he would order the liver.

"*Ciao*, hello," he said with an undisguised leer.

"You speak English?" I asked.

"Yes, and I would like to speak more and better."

"You work at the café, don't you?"

"Yes, it is my parent's bar. What would you like?"

Michael was so smitten he was stuttering.

"That, um, ah, *fegato* looks, um, utterly fabulous. I'm Michael, by the way," he said and held out his hand to her.

"I am Paula. How do you do?"

He started kissing her hand, making his way half way up her arm, mockingly, like some silly parody of an old Italian silent movie actor.

I looked at Marshall. The girl was probably no more than eighteen. He took Michael's arm.

"Actually, you hate liver, Michael, we'll find something else."

"But, but, but I do. I love liver!"

I shook my head at Paula ironically.

"It was very nice to meet you," she said, sharing my look, "You have bought the house at the bottom of this road, am I right?"

"Yes, we have," I answered as Marshall guided Michael firmly away.

"It is a very beautiful house."

I smiled and thanked her.

"Did you see her? Have you ever seen anything so, so

scrumptious!" Michael exclaimed as I caught up to them.

"Listen, old man, we have to live in this town," Marshall said, "And you don't know these people. A little advice. Take it easy on the girls."

"Oh, for God's sake, it isn't the middle ages!" Michael objected.

Suddenly Flavio spoke.

"I think you must be a little more discreet. In small villages there still exists a code, at least in public. Of course, in private it is something else."

I just laughed.

We made our way across the square and down another laneway beside the church where a stall was selling the specialty of the town, barbecued lamb kebabs. Flavio ordered the *arrosticini* for us.

"I must leave now. I am sorry I will miss the stilt walker but I am sure your friend will take many pictures for me. *Ciao*. It was very nice to meet you Michael. *Ciao,* you two friends. I will see you soon."

I got up and walked with Flavio back to the square.

"You must watch your friend," he said, "It is true. He does not understand about life in a small village. History is old but people change very little here."

"Don't worry. We'll take care of him. He doesn't mean any harm. He's a bit of a devil but that's what makes him charming."

When I returned to the table the food had arrived and Michael was digging in.

"God, this is delicious. What's it called? *Rostoconini?* Isn't that what you said?"

"No, *arrostocini!*"

After we had eaten I took Marshall by the arm and the

three of us made our way back up to the main square where the crowd had grown even larger. In one corner a clown was entertaining dozens of small children. And in another a few people were gathered around an accordionist and a flute player and in their midst a very old couple were dancing, moving around each other like two chickens, stamping and scratching the ground. The air was charged with sexuality between them.

It was dark now. Spotlights had come on in the square. Everyone was in excited anticipation. Suddenly there was a swell of music. Unlike anything I had heard before. Dissonant and clanging with a low drum beat going on beneath it.

The crowd fell silent as a huge bat-like creature appeared to fly in. A horrifying black monster almost twenty feet tall was taking huge strides across the cobblestones. Many of the children ran screaming to their parents. The people were all hugging the walls of the buildings to make space for this monstrous thing that flew back again, across the square and towards the church, swooping and dancing to the music. It seemed to claw itself half way up the church. Impossible! It must have been some amazing trick or there were wires I couldn't see. I looked at some of the faces around me and it wasn't awe I was seeing but fear. It sped back down the wall and darted menacingly at the people. Everyone kept moving farther away. It turned and started towards me. I was terrified, clinging to Marshall's arm.

"He's coming towards us!"

"He has to do something theatrical. You're not scared of him?"

"Yes, I am."

As he drew closer he opened his huge black wings and came to a sudden stop, not breathing, not moving, just hovering over us, his bulging face all black and bloated, and I screamed.

"Oh God, Marshall!"

Marshall thought the whole thing was marvelous! He was laughing and clapping and yelling "Bravo!" but the people just stared at him. They didn't applaud.

Michael, however, was in his element and never stopped filming. He managed to cover the entire piazza to get his footage.

I looked up at the monstrosity. A shiver went down my spine. The horrible visage was staring directly at me. I thought I was going to faint. I held onto Marshall's arm even tighter and shut my eyes. I could hear him laughing at me. When I opened them again the beast was no longer there, anywhere for that matter, he had disappeared.

"Where did he go?"

"Fantastic! Amazing performance. How the hell did he manage to create the effect on those two poles and stay on his feet on this cobblestone! Utterly fantastic!"

Michael rejoined us.

"I got it all. Bloody hell! I got it all!"

He wanted to show me some of the film on playback.

"Please, no, I don't want to see it. I've never been so scared in all my life! Where did he go?"

"He just vanished."

Michael was reloading his camera.

"What do you mean 'vanished'?" I asked.

"He just disappeared in a great big cloud of smoke! I've got it all here. Fantastic! Now where is that gorgeous Italian thing? I must get her on tape."

"Absolutely not, old man," Marshall answered sternly and we steered him home.

Needless to say we drank all the wine and then they started on the brandy so I left them to their own devices and went to bed. But I can tell you it was no easy sleep. If I thought I'd had nightmares before they didn't compare. The monstrous thing inhabited my dreams. It ate me, bled me, tortured me, killed me a hundred times. What a night!

When I got up the next morning I went quietly downstairs to make a cup of tea. No coffee this morning, the combination of the night and the alcohol had turned my stomach into a toxic wasteland. Tea would settle it I hoped. I opened the kitchen window and the town was silent as a tomb. I could only hear the birds and a dog that always barked in the distance. Even the bakery was shut. There were no delicious smells wafting into my kitchen. I heard some noise upstairs. They must be up, I thought, but the noise got louder. There was banging and doors slamming.

"Is Michael downstairs?" Marshall shouted.

"No!" I shouted back.

"Well, where the hell is he?"

"What do you mean? He's probably sleeping it off."

"In someone else's bed maybe because his is empty!"

Marshall came into the kitchen looking angry.

"He must have gone out early this morning while we were asleep," I said, trying to calm him down, "What did he whisper to you in the square last night."

"You know he was set on that girl. Wanted to take some video of her."

"You don't think he went out again last night and stayed out? With her?"

"She was too smart for that, I'm sure."

"Maybe something happened to him. He got mugged or got in a fight with someone."

"In this town? Who would hurt him? He certainly didn't have any money."

"There were lots of people who aren't from around here that were at the festival, hundreds of people."

"I'm going out to look for him."

"OK, but everything's closed except the bar."

Marshall left. Now I was really worried but I couldn't just sit and wait so I grabbed some laundry I had forgotten about and went upstairs to put it on the line. As I was pinning up the last shirt I thought I saw Michael down the end of the boulevard. He was staggering like a drunk in the middle of the road. Marshall was just leaving the bar and I called to him.

"Marshall, look down there!"

He started running towards Michael. I flew down the stairs and out the door. When I reached them Marshall was holding Michael in his arms. He was in terrible shape. His clothes were torn, he wasn't wearing his jacket and it did look as though he had been in a fight. There was a huge bruise on his forehead.

"Oh my god!" I said and reached over and touched his face.

He opened his eyes.

"Where the hell have you been?" demanded Marshall.

"I have no bloody idea," he said blankly and looked down at his filthy clothes, "Christ! What the hell happened to me?"

"We'd better get him inside," Marshall said.

Just at that moment the landlord of the bar arrived with a glass of brandy and gave it to Marshall.

"Grazie mille," he said and put the glass to Michael's lips. "Here, drink this."

Michael took a gulp and I handed the glass back to the landlord. We thanked him again and helped Michael to his feet. He kept repeating that he didn't feel good, that he must have drunk some home-made brew that nearly killed him.

As we entered the house the old lady was peering through her window again. I didn't have to look this time. I knew.

We laid Michael on the couch in the stone room and I got a blanket and a pillow and tried to make him comfortable.

"Let him rest for a few minutes. I'll make him a cup of tea."

Marshall sat with him while I went into the kitchen. I put the kettle on and got two aspirins and a glass of water. As I returned Michael was struggling to sit up.

"Lie back down, old man. You're a mess," Marshall said.

"Here, take these."

Michael took the aspirins and drank all the water.

"Thanks. What the hell? I mean, I have no idea what happened! The only thing I remember is walking and walking."

"Are you hurt anywhere?"

"No, I don't think so."

"Have you got your wallet?"

He checked in his trousers and pulled out his wallet. Marshall took it from him and looked inside.

"Seems like everything is there. Okay, let's start from the beginning."

"Where's your camera?" I asked Michael quietly.

"I must of lost it."

"Or it was stolen."

"Oh, yeah, the batteries were dead. Yes, now I remember. I went out into the town to see if I could find some. You know, maybe Angelo had some extras he would sell me."

"And then what happened?" Marshall asked.

"I went back up to the square to see if anyone was still there. And then, I don't know. I don't remember anything after that."

"Maybe a good hot tub will help."

Marshall got Michael to his feet and steadied him as they went upstairs.

"God, I feel so weak!"

"You'll be fine once you've had a bath and we've got some food in you."

"Yes, I'll warm some soup for him," I said and gestured to Marshall that he shouldn't let Michael lock the door or leave him alone.

"Okay, old man, here we go."

I went back to the kitchen and after about ten minutes Marshall came in.

"Forget the soup. He sat on the bed and rolled over and fell asleep. I'm going to put him on the first flight home in the morning. He should be checked by his doctor."

"Yes, I guess so. Did he tell you anything else?"

"He can't remember much. He went out looking for a battery. He went to the bar and asked Angelo and some of the locals. They bought him a few drinks. A little while later he left the bar and went across the square to get some air. A man was standing by the church door. He tried to make some conversation and that's it. From then on he doesn't know where he was or how he got on the road at the edge of town."

"Did he describe the man?"

"No. Nothing. Not even his name."

"I think you should go up to the bar and ask Angelo, maybe he knows something."

"They keep to themselves, you know, but maybe he saw something. I won't be long."

"Please. I don't want another disappearing act. Here, take the cell phone with you."

Marshall left and I went upstairs to check on Michael. The window was open and it was getting hot so I tiptoed to it and closed the shutters. His breathing was heavy but regular. I touched his forehead lightly. His skin was unusually cold.

Marshall returned a couple of minutes later.

"What did Angelo say?"

"Just what Michael told us. He had a few drinks then left. Angelo thought he was going home."

"So he didn't see who Michael was talking to in the square?"

"No, he said there wasn't anyone in the square. The other men left just after Michael and then Angelo closed up, went to his car and drove home."

"I checked on him. He felt very cold."

"Maybe it's just shock."

We spent the rest of the day quietly, looking in on Michael from time to time and each time he was sleeping soundly. Maybe he would remember something tomorrow. I realized I had the same feeling in my gut as the day we arrived.

FIVE

....

In the morning when I awoke, Marshall was already up. I could hear him clattering dishes downstairs and the water was running in the bathroom. I peeked into Michael's room. It was empty. I knocked on the bathroom door.

"Michael, are you in there?"

"Yes, my love?" he said cheerily, peeping his head out, "I'm just about done."

"How are you feeling?"

"Right as rain! Best night's sleep I've ever had!"

"Well, I'm glad."

"You're a darling!"

He came bouncing downstairs freshly dressed, shaved and packed.

"Kind of you two to bear with me. Sorry I was so wasted! Thank you but I can't say I won't be glad to get back to London. It's been lovely but after these eventful days I'll be happy to get back to my boring dull life and pusscat!"

There wasn't much time for anything but toast and coffee.

"And you still don't remember anything about the other night?"

It was very strange that he had never once mentioned or showed concern about the loss of his camera. It was totally unlike Michael.

"Not a thing. Didn't even dream. Slept like a baby! Sorry. God, I hope I wasn't too much trouble."

"Of course not."

I kissed him and wished him a safe flight.

"But if you ever find out what I was up to, you will let me know, won't you?" he said jokily, "Take care, darling. See you soon."

But I never did see Michael again. A few days after he arrived in London we got a call from his sister Marjorie saying he had been suddenly rushed to hospital and that the doctors were puzzled by his blood pressure which was inexplicably and dangerously low. The condition had seriously overtaxed his heart. I gave the phone to Marshall and they talked for some time and he noted down the telephone number of the hospital but we were too late. That night Michael died.

The English police called us the next morning to ask a few questions about Michael's activities while he was visiting us and we told them everything we knew. Marjorie was devastated and Marshall decided that he had to go and see her and do what he could to help her with the funeral. I agreed.

"But what about you?"

"Oh, I'll be fine."

I was lying of course.

"Well then, I'm calling Flavio. I would feel better if he knew you were on your own and checked in on you."

"Flavio is a busy man. Nothing is going to happen. I don't need the car. Leave it at the airport. You have your cell and you can call me anytime. Don't worry. I want to know about Michael. You will talk to the doctors, won't you?"

"Sure, but you have to promise me not to go up to that bar. Not at night. Okay?"

"I promise."

Neither of us slept very well and we were both relieved to get up the next morning. I fixed some sandwiches. Marshall refused to eat plane food. I made us some coffee and it was time to go. He was still reluctant until I promised again not to go up to the bar and to be sure to call Flavio.

"Yes. Yes, I will. Yes!"

I kissed him and sent him on his way.

In truth I was frightened. Not so much for the reasons Marshall thought but because without him I would have to cope. Sometimes shy people lean too heavily on those they love and trust.

Since I really had no intention of calling Flavio I was completely surprised when he landed on my doorstep.

"You look like you have seen a spirit! Didn't your husband tell you I was coming?"

"No, I just tried to ring him but I only got his answering message."

"He called me earlier this afternoon and told me what happened to your friend. I am so sorry. He asked me to come to you. So here I am and not only me," he said giggling, "But my night clothes too."

As usual he had brought two bottles of fine wine. We went into the kitchen and I got out some cheeses and a variety of sausage and olives.

"No cheese for me, thank you."

"You don't eat cheese? Impossible for an Italian. It's on everything!"

"Yes, it is okay if I don't see it."

"Flavio, you are funny."

"True. But now tell me about your friend, the Englishman."

"Oh, I forgot, I meant to check the email. Just to see if Marshall sent a message."

I opened my laptop and, yes, he had.

"He asks if you arrived," I said with a smile, "But no more

information on Michael and he'll call me tomorrow. Oh, here's a message from the professor. He thinks the box I gave him may date from sometime in the late 1800's but nothing yet on the contents."

"So, what about your friend?"

"He died of a heart attack."

"What happened when you found him?"

"We saw him stumbling up the road towards the house. He passed out in front of the bar."

"And he could not say where he went?"

"He couldn't remember a thing. We gave him some aspirins and he slept for the rest of the day and all the following night and in the morning he said he never felt better. Then we put him on the plane home. But his camera was stolen and the strangest thing of all was that he didn't seem to care about it."

"The true Latin lover, hm? I am sorry about the camera. Probably just a thief."

I wasn't listening to him. For some reason I was thinking again about the designs I had seen on the chapel door in the little church in the square.

"A penny for your thoughts."

"Those symbols on my dining room ceiling."

"What about them?"

"There are the same symbols in the church."

"Really?"

"Let's go up to the square. I want to show you before the church closes. Maybe Angelo will know something."

As we stepped outside, I saw a young boy at the old woman's door. She was handing him something wrapped in brown paper and, at the sight of us, he tore off up the laneway. The old woman closed the door quickly. I felt another cold chill go up my spine.

The town was oddly deserted except for a few old men in the bar playing *briscola* and drinking their aperitifs. Angelo was sitting with them reading a newspaper. The men stopped their card game and were very quiet. Normally when they played they would be shouting at each other and nothing could distract them. They nodded to Flavio, almost in deference. He politely answered their gesture with the word, *"Sera."*

We sat at a vacant table and Angelo got up and came to us and I introduced him to Flavio again, thinking that he might not remember him from the night of the festival but he did and they shook hands.

Flavio ordered two glasses of wine. I took out some sample drawings I had made of the designs from my pocket.

"Maybe he knows what these mean."

"I am in doubt but we can ask."

Angelo brought the wine and we invited him to sit down. Flavio took the paper and showed the drawings to him and asked if he recognized them. He put on his glasses and looked at them carefully for a long time and then at me and then shook his head and muttered something to Flavio in Italian.

"He has never seen them before," Flavio translated, "He also said we must finish our drinks. He is closing early. His son's wife is in hospital to have a baby and there are complications and he must go."

Flavio paid for our drinks and we left. Outside the square was totally empty. We approached the little church. I was glad to find the door open and we went inside.

"We stood by this church on the night of the *festa*," Flavio said.

"Yes, but you haven't seen what I want to show you now."

"We need light."

"No, the candles are lovely. Look over there. We can light a few more."

"Then you must make an indulgence and pay for forgiveness."

"I know. Have you got any change?"

"Spiccioli, sì."

"I'll light one and ask for forgiveness if that will make you feel better."

"No, you will feel better because God will bless you. And for some reason I think it is necessary for blessing."

"Are you frightened?"

"No, not exactly, but it is always good to take precaution."

Flavio followed me to the side chapel and I pointed out the same beautiful symbols within the grating that were painted on my dining room ceiling.

Flavio tried the handle of the carved metal door.

"No, Flavio, what are you doing?"

"Seeing if it is open."

He pulled and it opened and we went in. I felt jittery as though I was committing a sin, crossing private property. We could see the corpse encased in glass in the dim red glow.

"That is the body of Sister Beata Maria della Palombara," I told him.

"I see, yes, very well preserved."

Suddenly we both heard a snap. The door had closed behind us and when I tried to open it again it wouldn't budge.

"Flavio, the door is stuck."

"Let me try."

He pulled and pulled.

"Not stuck. It is locked."

"Oh, my god."

"Now do not be scared."

He took a credit card from his wallet and tried several

times to slide it down and flick the lock open but it was no use.

"Now this is the modern age. Do not get excited," Flavio said and pulled out his cell phone, "Who can we call that you know in this town?"

"Oh dear, um, I only know the number of the pizzeria."

"We will try. Okay?"

"Um, 333-031-3309."

Flavio dialed.

"It is not working."

"Maybe it's, um, wait, 333-301. Or try the bar. No, it's closed."

"You do not understand. The phone does not work in this church."

"Well, someone must be coming to lock up soon. I can't believe the phone doesn't work!"

"You are right. For now we just sit and wait calmly."

"There's nowhere to sit."

Flavio hopped up and sat on the altar.

"Flavio, that's sacrilege!"

"What is God's belongs to his people. I am his people and I am fatigued of standing."

Flavio looked inside the ciborium which usually contains the host but it was empty. Then he started pushing everything on the altar aside.

"Flavio, stop it! What would the nuns say if they saw you?"

"They would say that I was a bad boy and send me to confession. I would confess my sin and then be absolved and *presto!* I would be good again!"

Flavio was trying to move a copper orb that was set in the marble and we heard a heavy grinding noise. A large area of the tiled floor was shifting sideways, uncovering a staircase that led down into the bowels of the church. I wondered how many bodies had been thrown into this crypt!

"What was this for?"

"Ah, yes. Well, this would probably be a secret passageway for the priests," Flavio said and shone his cell phone light down into the passage. "Yes, it is very old, a secret hiding place for example during bad times, maybe?"

I peered down into the dark dank hole and the smell emanating from it was awful.

"It probably has not been opened for many years," Flavio observed.

"I'd say so."

"Come. We will see!"

"Are you crazy? You don't know what's down there."

"Do you have a better idea how we will get out of here?"

"No."

I took out my lighter and lit two candles from the altar and handed one to Flavio.

"Good idea. I now am glad you smoke but only for this moment. You must quit that horrible habit."

"This is no time to preach."

"You are right. Well, shall I go first?"

"Please."

"Do not be frightened. There is probably an exit that must go under the square out to the street."

"You hope."

"I am always full of hope when there is adventure. Hope is the reason for life!"

As we descended the marble staircase I noticed that it was in terrible condition. Many of the slabs were broken or missing completely and it was also extremely narrow which brought on my claustrophobia.

"Please be careful," Flavio warned, "The stairs are precarious."

I followed him as closely as I could but the shadows were so deep that at one point I missed a step and fell backwards.

"Ooow!"

"Do not do that, *carina*, marble is very hard on the ass!"

"No kidding."

My claustrophobia was getting worse and I started to hyperventilate.

"Flavio, I can't do it. It's too narrow. Oh my God!"

"Close your eyes. I will be your Virgil and guide you to the bottom."

I laughed a little and a bit of the fear left me.

"Now we go, all right?"

"All right."

I closed my eyes and took Flavio's hand and we moved down very slowly.

"Here we are," Flavio said, "But there isn't much to see."

I opened my eyes. There were no openings or windows. It was nothing more than a cavern hewn out of the bedrock and the floor was dirt.

"Well? I don't see any way of getting out of here. Let's go back," I said, shaking a little from the cold and damp, not to mention terror.

"Maybe this is just a secret room with no exit."

"That would be impractical. Priests would not have built an exit with no exit."

He began to move about the cavern.

"Italians understand the art of escape. They have had centuries of practice. No, there must be some way out."

As he moved his candle kept flickering. I was careful to protect mine.

"You see, there is air moving in here. We follow it and we find an exit."

He placed his hands on the dusty wall and moved them up and down while he made a complete circle.

"Here I have found it."

The top of the opening was no more than four feet above the floor. Flavio bent down and shone the candlelight into the hole.

"In there?" I exclaimed.

"All right, I will go in alone and see how far it is."

"Oh Flavio, I feel like an idiot. I'll try and do it."

"No, it will not help to have you in back of me gasping and fainting. Once I know there is a way out then you can do it."

"You will be careful?"

"Of course, I am a coward. Believe me if there is even one rat in this hole I will return and we go back to the church."

"Okay, go on. I'll be all right."

"You have more courage than you know, *carina*. There is nothing here to be frightened of."

As Flavio crawled into the infernal black hole he began to whistle. I could see that it would be next to impossible for him to turn around in such a cramped and narrow passageway. I began to feel dizzy and sat down on the hard cold ground.

As I did a strong breath of wind flew through the room and blew my candle out. I searched in my pockets for the lighter but it wasn't there. What now? I sat in complete darkness and the only thing I could hear was Flavio's whistling disappearing at an alarming rate and the sound of my own heart pounding in my eardrums.

Flavio could not have been gone for more than a couple of minutes but it seemed like an eternity. In complete stillness and darkness one's mind can play such strange tricks that I actually

thought something was in there with me and I was very
relieved to hear Flavio shuffling back through the tunnel. I
couldn't see him since he too had lost his candlelight.

"Are you there, *carina?*"

"Yes."

"I hope you have your lighter."

"No, I must have dropped it on the stairs."

I could hear him brushing off his pants.

"Yes, well, now we will have to make our way in blackness.
It will be the blind leading the blind."

"Oh God!"

"He will not give us light, I can assure you, so we must do
the best we can. You follow me and we will feel our way along
the passage."

"So there is a way out?"

"Of course. Come. There is, as you use in metaphor, light
at the end of the tunnel. So don't be afraid, *carina.*"

I got to my feet and found him in the dark. He entered first
and I took a deep breath and followed. It was probably the
tightest space I had ever been in my life and I thought if I
could get through this without passing out I might never need
a therapist again. All I can say is that I was thankful that the
tunnel was not as long as I had expected.

It opened into another larger cavern and there was
moonlight streaming in through a metal grate about twelve feet
above our heads.

"Oh, thank God!" I said with great relief.

"Do you not see a problem?"

"No, we just push that grate out and climb onto the street."

"Yes, *carina,* and where is the ladder?"

"Oh, shit. Well, come on then, if we both yell loud enough
I know someone will hear."

"You are the actress. You yell."

I let out the most piercing stage scream I could muster.

"That was not bad, *carina*. Maybe you are in the wrong career. Maybe you should have been an opera singer."

"Oh, shut up. Come on, the two of us can make it even louder."

So, despite Flavio's reluctance, we set to a variety of howls and shouts and in no more than a few minutes we heard voices from above.

"*Che successo!*" someone called down into the cavern.

Flavio responded in Italian and there was a lot more yelling and talking as other townsfolk arrived on the scene and helped remove the grate.

"Are they going to get us out?"

"Of course. They are bringing a ladder from a neighbor.

"Oh, good."

"Well, it is not so good."

"What are you saying?"

"The police are very angry. We are trespassing. They want to talk to us as for why we are here."

"Oh no!"

"Oh yes. I have never liked the *carabinieri*. Especially when they are not pleased."

"Well, they can't arrest us."

He didn't reply.

"Can they?"

"The *carabinieri* can do anything."

A few moments later a ladder was sent down to us. Flavio told me to go first. I reached the top and paused for a second. The policeman was very large and very tall and I could see lots of gold teeth as he sneered at me.

"Signora," he said in a low voice as he offered me his hand.

Then Flavio climbed up and spoke to him and turned to me.

"They are taking us to the local station."

"I never heard anything so ridiculous. We aren't criminals."

"No, but you are *una straniera*."

"So? I live here. They know that."

"Yes, but they do not know that you are a kind, sensitive, good citizen. So they will ask some questions. Do not worry, *carina*. Remember that I am a lawyer and remember I do all the talking."

There were three policeman now and they told us to follow them and we went down through the square past the lower church and beyond the old town to the station. A few of the villagers were standing outside their doorways, no doubt wondering what all the commotion and yelling had been about. I recognized one woman who I had met during the *festa* and she smiled and waved. I smiled back a little sheepishly.

At the police station we were told to wait in a small room and after a little while a fourth *carabiniere* entered. He was obviously the chief and, contrary to the others, he seemed very friendly. He even spoke a little English to me but I tried to keep my answers to a minimum as Flavio had instructed. It only took a few minutes and the interview was over. The chief stood up and bowed to me.

"I am very sorry for this," he said pleasantly, "Your lawyer has been very good. You can go. But, Signora, I must ask you not to say about what has happened to anyone or there may be some problem for you."

I was a little taken aback at the remark but his manner was kindly and I shook his hand. As we reached the door he asked-

"You like our little town?"

"Oh yes, very much."

"Good, good. It is peaceful here."

Outside the other *carabinieri* were leaning against their police car, smoking. Flavio went over to them and shook their hands and thanked them for their trouble and their help.

We left the station and started walking back around the town on the lower road to the house and we could hear disco music playing.

"Where is that coming from?" Flavio asked.

"Rosaria, the woman who runs the pizza parlor, puts on outdoor disco parties for the young people, in a little park that is just below our house. I forgot there was one tonight. Three weeks ago it ended at four in the morning and kept us awake the whole time."

As we walked further there were cars parked all along the roadside and in the distance hundreds of young people milling about. We approached the park and I saw Rosaria.

"*Ciao*, Rosaria! Looks like it is going well."

She spoke perfect English. She had been born in Canada and spent ten years there as a child before her family decided to return to Montevecchio.

"Come on in!" she said.

"Do you want to, Flavio?"

"But of course! I love discos!"

"You do?"

"Yes, I go all the time."

"You never cease to amaze me."

"Rosaria, this is my good friend Flavio."

They greeted each other and Rosaria gave us wristbands.

"What should we pay?"

"Don't worry about it, just go in and have a good time. The bar is over there."

"Thanks."

We made our way towards the bar. I couldn't believe there were so many people. We had to elbow a path. Rosaria was yelling at the bartender to serve us but he couldn't hear over the loud music so she pushed through the crowd and got behind the bar and made drinks for us herself.

"You have much influence in this town," Flavio whispered to me.

"Don't be silly. Thanks, Rosaria."

"Have fun!" she said and disappeared into the crowd.

Flavio and I made our way towards the dance floor. It was packed but Flavio pulled me onto it anyway.

"No, Flavio!"

"Come, *carina*. We make just one dance and then we go home."

We started to dance and got separated in the crush of people. I looked around but I couldn't see Flavio anywhere. It was like he had just disappeared. I was pushing my way back towards the bar through the dancing horde when suddenly a young man stepped in front of me.

"Piace ballare, Signora?"

He was the most beautiful man I had ever seen. He wore a long dark coat and a white scarf. His eyes were the most brilliant blue and held me spellbound as he put his arm around my waist and twirled me round and round, faster and faster. I felt as though I were floating above the floor then, as quickly as he had appeared, he vanished and I could see Flavio standing on the sidelines.

"Where did you disappear to? Did you see that strange boy?"

"I was needing to use the bathroom."

"You just left me and then some strange boy asked me to dance. Didn't you see him?"

"No, I only hope he was as good a dancer as me!"

"He was beautiful. He had the bluest eyes I've ever seen."

"Did you ever notice him before?"

"No. Let's go, Flavio, I'm really very tired."

The minute we came in the door I poured two stiff brandies and handed one to Flavio.

"I never drink anything but wine but this is exception. Thank you."

We sat at the kitchen table and for a moment neither of us spoke.

"Excuse me," I said, "I want to check if there's a message from Marshall. I need to know if he's all right."

As I went up the two flights I turned on every light there was. When I opened the email there was nothing.

I returned to the kitchen to find Flavio with his head in the refrigerator.

"What are you looking for?"

"Food, of course, I am so very hungry," he said, taking out a slice of sausage, "May I?"

"Yes, please go ahead. But how can you be hungry after all this?"

"Because my stomach is telling me to eat. Would you like some?"

"No, I want you to tell me everything you said to the policeman at the station and what he said to you."

"Absolutely not," he replied coyly, breaking off a large chunk of baguette.

"Why not?" I exclaimed, infuriated.

"Because you must live in this town now. You know a lawyer must keep his mouth shut."

"Did he threaten you?"

He paused, finishing his mouthful. I handed him a napkin.

"In one word? Yes."

"Why that's against the law."

"*Mia carina*, he is the law. Certainly in this town. And I am a lawyer, so I know. And I am Italian, so I know. You must not speak of this to anyone."

"Okay, I won't."

Flavio laughed.

"Oh, you forget I know you. You cannot keep a secret."

"What a thing to say."

"Is it true or no?"

I looked at him silently and then had to admit it.

"Yes, it's true."

He put down his plate of sausage and bread and leaned towards me and put his hands on my shoulders.

"All I can tell you is this. You must not . . never . . speak of it to anyone in this town. What you say to Marshall, or when you go home, that is your business. But not here."

"Flavio, this is ridiculous. All we did was get locked in the church and try and find our way out of there. What is so bad about that?"

"I do not know," he answered and resumed eating his meal, "What may seem innocent to you apparently is not innocent to the police."

"What did they say to you?"

He looked at me sternly.

"I will only tell you that you have been warned."

"Oh, my God, this is too bizarre."

"True. It is. But I am tired now. I will take my pajamas and toothbrush if you will show me my room."

"You aren't seriously going to sleep now?"

"Of course. I am tired and I think you are too."

"Flavio, but . . "

"Never mind. We will sleep now and talk *domani*."

"How can you be so practical? I can't possibly go to sleep."

"Oh, you will see. You do not know how tired you are."

"Well, I'm not! All this stuff happening, one thing after another. All this . . "

I couldn't find the words.

"Adventure? Intrigue?"

"No." I found the word. "Drama! Centuries of drama!"

"Are you sure it is us who makes the drama, *carina?*"

"Oh, never mind, go on. Your room is next to the bathroom."

"*Grazie.* Sleep well, my Lady. And please, *carina,* no sleepwalking, I am very tired."

Again he had made me laugh and I was grateful for that.

No sooner had Flavio gone upstairs and I finished the last swallow of my brandy than I realized how tired I really was. The minute I put my head on the pillow I was out cold.

SIX

....

The morning was especially beautiful. 'It must be late,' I thought, 'if the sun is so warm'. I looked over at the clock. Yes, it was almost nine in the morning. Then I smelt the coffee. I got up and threw on my housecoat and went downstairs.

Flavio had made coffee, already gone to the bakery and come back with a lovely fresh baguette and there he was scrambling some eggs.

"Sleep well, *carina?*"

"You were right, I went out like a light. When did you get up?"

"Only a few hours ago. I thought you would need some food."

He put the plate of eggs in front of me and poured me a lovely espresso.

"Mmmm, looks good, thank you."

He sat down with his plate and coffee.

"Now, *carina*, I must leave soon for the office. Will you be all right?"

"Oh, sure."

'But would I?' I thought. What was Marshall up to? No emails, no phone calls. I wanted to tell him what had happened.

"When is Marshall to come home?"

"The day after tomorrow, I think."

Flavio noticed that I wasn't eating my eggs.

"What is wrong, *carina?*"

"Oh, nothing. Maybe I'm still a little nervous about the whole thing."

"Oh, I see. Well, I have a better plan. How about I do not leave you here to think too much. You come with me. We will drop by my office for a moment and then I will take you home with me. My mother wants to meet you. I have told her much about you."

"Oh no Flavio, I couldn't do that. You must have lots of things to do."

"No, no, it is a good idea. I think Marshall would be much happy to know that I have not left you alone after such a night. There is something I want to show you at my estate. Now finish your food. I must call the office. Then you dress and this time you bring your toothbrush, *sì?*"

I nodded, smiling at him gratefully. It was true, I would just brood.

"Yes, okay. Thank you. I won't be long."

I dashed upstairs and got in the shower and dressed quickly, bringing down only my night bag.

"Ready."

"Good."

We opened the door and again that small face peered at us through her shuttered window. I looked at her bravely and proudly, knowing she must be thinking that some immoral hanky-panky was going on.

Flavio's family estate was not opulent or grand. It was more like a little *borgo*. A few scattered ruins that were in the process of being restored and a large new house where he lived with his mother and father and an occasional uncle. The surrounding land and rolling hills and valleys were serene and situated on a mountain slope above the Tronto river.

After meeting Flavio's mother, and leaving her to prepare lunch, he insisted that we go for a walk. It was mostly a path through woodland but soon we came upon a clearing and Flavio pointed out a ruin sitting perfectly perched on the top of a knoll. It was the size of a small castle.

"There is the home of my wizard uncle."

"Is he still alive?"

"Ooh, *certo no!* He lived one hundred years ago. He died there. And no one has lived there since."

"Why? It belongs to your family, doesn't it?"

"Well, in a way, yes. Part of it belongs to my mother." He pointed in the distance. "The other part belongs to relatives to whom we do not speak. They own the land but not the castle and I cannot restore the castle because I cannot cross their land."

"Then what are we doing here?"

"What are they going to do? Shoot me? No, *carina,* but they can go to the *comune* to stop my restorations. My mother and I always walk here. This is where she finds the *porcini* you love so much. In October I will bring you to my mother and you will hunt."

"Oh, that would be wonderful, Flavio. I'm crazy about mushrooms. I remember as a little girl picking hundreds of mushrooms, filling garbage bags full of them. When my parents were tired they sent me out to get more and more. I returned with so many that my fingertips had turned black from picking. But they weren't *porcini.* They were called *myszlaki* in Polish."

"It is a funny language, Polish, all those sh-sh-shs."

"Now Flavio, every language is funny when you don't speak it, even Italian."

He laughed and took my arm.

"Come, we must hurry, lunch will be ready soon."

We reached the castle ruins. Most of the interior walls were still standing and you could get an idea of the layout.

"When did he die? Did he live here alone? Or did he have a family?"

"No, he never married. He was murdered. Or so the people say. They never found his body. My family believes he was murdered because he claimed to be a wizard and the church put a curse on him. But my grandmother used to tell me a story about this great uncle. He was well educated. He had been sent to Milan to study philosophy at the university and was to enter the holy order of the Franciscans but halfway through his study he left and began traveling throughout Europe. When his money ran out and the family would no longer support him he came here to this small castle and lived alone for the rest of his life."

"What did he do here? All alone?"

"He bought one of the libraries of antiquity and had all the books sent here."

"He just read?"

"He did not only reading. He was trying to find a way to eternal life."

"Like women today trying to find the fountain of youth."

"In a way," he said and laughed. "My grandmother told me that he became a vampire."

"What? That's just legend. Lots of people believe in vampires. Even my own grandmother believed in them. I could never get her to realize it was just a superstition based on ignorance."

"Are you sure of that?"

"Flavio, don't tell me you believe your uncle was a

vampire."

"My grandmother had been severely warned to never go near the castle. But, like most little girls she was curious, and one day she slipped out of the house and knocked on his front door. When he answered, she told me he was very angry. He told her to go home and that unless she wanted to stay there forever with him she should never come again."

"That doesn't prove he was a vampire just a miserable old man. If you and your family believe in vampires then you know they don't die so he couldn't have been murdered. He must still be alive or whatever you call it."

Despite my disbelief, I shivered slightly.

"What is the matter, *carina*? Something walked on your back?" Flavio laughed again. "You are right, it is only a story. But come, Mama does not like to wait."

Flavio's mother had prepared a tray of beautiful little sandwiches but she herself didn't eat anything. She treated Flavio with the deference customary for an only male child and soon left us to ourselves. I thanked her and she smiled at me and, at the same time, winked at Flavio.

"Mamma! È sposata!"

His mother shrugged at me in polite apology and left, looking slightly disappointed.

"She is always hopeful."

"Of what?"

"Oh, that I will marry and give her ten grandchildren. What else?"

He seemed distant for one brief moment.

"I can see she is very proud of you. You are restoring her old village and you have a very successful law firm. And you take good care of them."

"You know how it is in Italy, *'la famiglia'* is all, and they have no one else but me. I am very lucky. My clothes are cleaned, I have good meals and with all this I also have my freedom."

Yes, I thought. He was lucky but for other reasons.

Why did all Italian children want to stay with their families, if not in the home, at least within spitting distance until well into their thirties and even forties and sometimes for the rest of their lives? Whereas we can't wait to get out of the house and away from our parents. Then, when it's too late, we come back home to see them, aged and crippled and lonely. And they look at us with sadness and a touch of recrimination because all we brought home was our own guilt. I was one of those children. Their faces haunt me still.

I realized how much I envied Flavio. I envied the care he had taken with his aging parents. I envied the fact that he had always known he would never abandon them.

Flavio's mother brought in a pot of coffee and he poured it, adding two large cubes of sugar into his tiny cup. Italians like their coffee sweet.

Afterwards he left me to my own devices and returned to his office. There wasn't much to do and, since I couldn't easily converse with his mother, I decided to take another walk. I knew that October was for *porcini* but I also knew it was the season for other mushrooms like chanterelles and parasols. I must have walked for about an hour when I came to the end of the wood and there it was again . . the castle! I had somehow come upon it from a different angle. I had to squint because in that direction the sun was blinding but I know I saw someone, just for a split second, climb over a wall and disappear into the ruin.

Every time Marshall and I had gone to explore Italy's gorgeous countryside, when we thought there could not be a soul around, it never failed that someone appeared out of nowhere and this time was no exception.

When I got back to Flavio's house he was waiting on the porch.

"*Carina,* where have you been?" he asked rather seriously.

"Just walking. I went down through the woods again on a different path but I still came across your uncle's castle. I must have made a complete circle. I took the shorter route home. The one we walked this morning."

Flavio didn't say anything but came towards me and put his hand on my shoulder.

"Well, I am glad you have returned. You know, *carina,* there are times you make me worried."

"Why?"

"I think you are someone who has the fortune or misfortune to have strange experiences happen to them. But never mind. I have made a plan for us to have dinner with some friends at my favorite restaurant tonight. Is that good?"

"Oh sure, that's great."

"But first I want to show you our restored theater. It is over two hundred years old. They are performing Romeo and Juliet. It is a traveling company."

"Can we see it?"

"No, they are not playing tonight so I can show you the theater. I am on the board for the restorations."

We changed and Flavio's mother brought us a small glass of cordial. It was the most delicious thing I had ever tasted. It was a liqueur made from walnuts. Apparently it was a very old recipe that had been in the family for years. Flavio's mother collected the walnuts from the same woods I had explored that afternoon. Then she pressed the inside lining of the shells together with the nuts which produced a syrup to which she would add some secret spices. It was bottled and kept in the cellar for years to age. It was a dark amber liquid, a little thicker than brandy and much stronger. She poured not much more than a thimbleful into beautifully-cut tiny crystal glasses. I asked her why she didn't join us but she only shook her head and said that it was too strong and only for special guests. You couldn't feel the effect immediately but as we got in the car my head began to spin a little.

"Wow, that is powerful stuff."

"Yes, like your Polish *spiritus*, no?"

We drove into the lovely Roman city of Ascoli Piceno which was only fifteen minutes from Flavio's house. He took us up through the steepest part of the town to a piazza at the very top. We parked the car and got out in front of a small building with a sign saying, *'Teatro Novello'.*

"Here it is. Our beautiful little theater. Come, I have a key. We go in."

It was a small proscenium theater in the traditional horseshoe shape. It maybe held two hundred people but it was 'delicious'. The seating was plush red in three tiers with lovely archways. The ceiling was painted with frescoes of doves and angels. When Flavio turned on the switch, a beautiful crystal chandelier overhead gave off a brilliant light.

"Oh, Flavio, this is just magnificent."

"Yes, it is. Come, I will show you behind."

We walked down the aisle and then up a few steps onto the stage. I turned and looked out into the auditorium. I felt like I was home again. I thought of what might have happened here over the centuries . . what plays were performed, who were the leading actors of the time. I recalled my first professional experience, almost thirty years since, and sighed.

"I would like to see you play Lady Macbeth here," Flavio whispered behind me.

"Oh no, Flavio, that was long ago."

"I am sure you have not forgotten."

"No, but it's better left in my mind."

"Just a few lines. For me, *carina*?"

It had been a very long time but the nerves . . I remembered them well.

I did one of Lady Macbeth's short speeches from early in the play when she begs the devil to take her soul, to transform her into a man so that she could commit a murder without remorse or guilt. The thrill of doing it though was accompanied with embarrassment. As if I were once again a young girl auditioning for a director that I admired and was terrified of. My impulse was always to run for the exit.

Flavio came down the aisle and jumped onto the stage. He took my hand and kissed it.

"I now understand what your husband was meaning, *carina*. Maybe one day I will be lucky to see you play the whole."

"No Flavio, this all you get."

"Why have you left the stage?"

"Because there comes a time for some actors in their career when you feel you are pretending and in that moment the mask falls slightly and there it is, that third eye watching your every move and you realize the magic is gone."

"Ahh, I understand you," he said wistfully. "Come, I will show where the actors live."

We went backstage to the dressing rooms. They were very tiny. We sat down in the largest of the three and Flavio explained more about the current touring production and the actors who were performing.

"It is played by only men."

"Do they dress up as women?" I asked.

"No, they put on very simple tunics over their own clothes.

You see here is a photo of Romeo and Juliet."

I looked at the photo and gasped. Romeo was a tall thin man in his forties and Juliet was in his sixties with a cropped white beard and shoulder-length hair.

"Juliet has a beard?"

"Yes."

"But she's only fifteen."

"But he believes he is Juliet, a young girl in pain and in love. Does he not understand the ecstasy and loss of love best?"

"They must be marvelous actors."

"It is surprisingly effective."

We only had to walk around the corner to the restaurant.

"It is called *'C'era una volta'*. It has been here for many years. The woman who did all the cooking is dead now but her son has continued. It is, how you say, *paesano?*"

"It sounds great. I'm hungry."

"Come, my friends are already waiting for you."

It was a wonderful evening. The food was superb. We had *antipasti*, a dish with tripe cooked in tomatoes and herbs, a boar's meat pasta and liver cooked with egg and there was roast lamb and even a *porcini* risotto to die for. The dessert was my new found favorite, *panna cotta*. It was the best I had ever tasted, so light and creamy and topped with fresh *frutta di bosco*. A cup of strong espresso completed an absolutely fantastic meal. I was so high from the energy of the people and their laughter and love of food and conversation that I thought I would never leave this country.

We got home well after midnight. I thanked Flavio and was so wonderfully tired that I slept like a log.

In the morning the Signora served a delicious cappuccino and a brioche and Flavio drove me back to Montevecchio.

He dropped me at the front door. As I gave him a kiss on the cheek the old woman was watching. 'She probably thinks I'm having affair with our lawyer,' I thought. It was like living in a goldfish bowl. I gave Flavio another big kiss on the other cheek.

"What will the neighbors say?" he teased.

"What they always say . . who is that marked woman!"

He laughed and I got out and went inside.

I immediately opened my email to see if Marshall had left a message. He had sent one the previous evening.

'No more news about Michael. It was a massive heart attack. Marjorie is devastated but knows there is little I can do. I was going to stay for the funeral but I met a man on the plane here, an Italian publisher, who is interested in my book. He wants me to meet with him in Rome the day after next. So I've booked to fly back tomorrow morning. I get in to Pescara at noon. I could just pick up the car and drive straight to Rome on the *autostrada* but why don't I come and get you?'

I sat back and thought about it. He'd be on the plane now but, of course, he would call before he decided what to do. I was checking the time, just after eleven, when another email came up. It was from the professor.

'Gentile Signora, can you come to Firenze? If possible tomorrow? I have strange news and it is necessary for you to be here for me to show something to you.'

Tomorrow! Florence! I had no idea how to get to Florence except that it was about a three or four hour drive from Montevecchio. I wasn't sure what to do so I emailed Flavio.

'I know this is short notice but Marshall is arriving in Pescara at noon and has to go to Rome for a meeting with a publisher he met on the way to London. I was going to go with him but the professor just sent an email asking that I come to Florence tomorrow because he has something important to show me. I know this is asking too much but would it be possible for you to come with me?'

I sent the email and before I even had time to shut down my laptop the phone rang.

"But yes, *carina,* of course. I will drive you. I love Firenze."

"But what about work?"

"There is nothing that is so important. I will be at your house tomorrow morning at seven."

"So early?"

"We must. As long as we return the same day it is perfectly possible. Tell the professor we will meet with him at 11:30."

"Oh, you are a saint!"

"Not yet, not yet."

"See you in the morning."

I emailed the professor and waited for Marshall to call, which he did an hour later. I told him everything that had happened and he agreed to go to Rome without me. He thought he might have to spend two nights in the hotel there because Signor del Credi, the publisher, had invited him to have dinner with some colleagues the following evening. It was very exciting for him and I wished him luck and told him how much I loved him.

That night it was difficult to sleep and I was awake long before seven and had showered and dressed and eaten breakfast. I was so fidgety I took a walk down into the square below to get some air and watch the sunrise. The bar was just opening and I went in and ordered a coffee. The *barista,* Paula's mother, seemed amazingly cheerful at this early hour but as she didn't speak a word of English I just smiled and took my coffee to an outside table. I could feel the warmth of the sun even though it was barely peeping over the top of the mountains. There was a newspaper on the table where I sat and I flipped through it. It was the regional paper from Ascoli and, as I turned the first few pages, I came across an article that mentioned Montevecchio and beside it a picture of a very old man with long white hair holding a basket over his arm. He was smiling.

'Local man found dead in the Sibillini near the *rifugio*,' the heading said. The *rifugio* was a high viewpoint and entry to a climbing area in the mountains. It also had a place to park your car and a small restaurant. Apparently he had been hunting for mushrooms and was found dead. There were no signs of violence but if the public had any information they were asked to please call the police. They gave the name of the old man but it didn't ring any bells.

Later there was mention of a young man, very tall and wearing a long overcoat, who had been seen in the area and what was most unusual and the reason the witness had remembered him was that he had leapt from a rocky ledge at a great height and landed safely below before disappearing. I thought of the figure I had seen at the castle and wondered if it could have been the same person. The police were looking for this man and asked that anyone else who might have seen him to please contact them. I wondered if I should.

Flavio's car came up the boulevard and he rolled down his window.

"You are ready?"

"Yes, just wait. I made some sandwiches."

The bar was only yards from the house so I ran back and quickly grabbed the paper bag with our lunch and my purse.

"Whew! Sorry. I was up so early this morning I thought I'd have a coffee at the bar. You're exactly on time."

"Aren't I always?"

I hopped in and showed him what I had brought.

"Ah, *brava!* No cheese?"

"No cheese."

I realized I still had the newspaper in my hands. I folded it into the bag and off we went.

SEVEN

....

"I love driving," Flavio said as we roared along.

On the way I told Flavio a little more about Marshall's publisher and that his name was Paulo del Credi.

"Have you heard of him?"

"No, I do not think so," Flavio answered.

"It would be wonderful for Marshall if it happened. It's very hard to get a publisher these days. If it's published in Italian then that may get an English publisher interested."

"That is nice. How long will he be staying in Rome?"

"Signor del Credi is taking Marshall out for dinner tomorrow night with some business partners and he'll be home the day after."

We didn't talk much for the rest of the journey. Only about the amazing places that we passed. Assisi, Perugia, Lake Trasimene, Cortona, Arezzo. We finally turned off the *autostrada* and into a tiny *borgo* and stopped in front of a little café.

"We will have our *tramezzini* here, *bene*? I am starving."

"Yes, fine."

Flavio ordered two coffees and we sat outside eating our sandwiches.

"How far are we from Florence?" I asked.

"Not so far, about forty-five kilometers, but I thought it is a nice place to stop. It is very curious that the professor didn't say what he was wanting you to see."

"He wouldn't say anything except that it was urgent to

come as soon as possible."

"I wonder what it could be? Maybe he has found out about the copper box and the origin of the contents."

As we drank our coffee I showed him the photo in the newspaper.

"Look at this. It's about a man from Montevecchio who was found dead up by the *rifugio*. Could you tell me exactly what it says? "

I pointed to the article and noticed Flavio demeanour suddenly change. It was odd.

"Is anything wrong?"

He took the paper and quickly glanced over the article.

"Hmm, obviously he was so old he died of a heart failure."

"Yes, I suppose so. Does it say anything else?"

"No."

He stood up and straightened his collar, then casually walked over and threw the newspaper and the sandwich wrappings in the garbage.

"Come, we must go or we will be late."

It's against the law to drive through the center of Florence unless you have a special permit and there is nowhere to park but Flavio knew the city well and took us down some incredibly narrow and congested streets to a garage that was very close to the university and right at the edge of the *centro storico*. We left the car there and set off in the direction of the professor's office. Marshall and I had visited Florence the year before so its beauty and quaintness were no surprise to me.

"We came here for four days last year. As a matter of fact we stayed right there at that *albergo*," I said, pointing to a tiny hotel just around the corner from the garage.

"I believe that you have seen more of Italy than any Italian."

"We went to Sicily a few months ago. Strange place. Nothing like Le Marche, is it?"

"I do not know. I have never been to Sicily."

"What? Never?"

"No, never. Actually most Italians who live in the north never venture to the south. They think it is not really Italy but another country."

"But Flavio, Italy was unified in the 19th century," I said teasingly.

"True, but not in the hearts of most Italians."

We were now in the very center of the city.

"Look, Flavio," I said, parading my knowledge, "That's where the monk Savonarola lived while he was in Florence."

"Yes, I know, *carina*. The man who almost toppled the corrupt papal authority in the 15th century. It is also where my great-uncle studied to be a monk. He believed very much what Savonarola believed."

"Really? Then why did he leave?"

"Maybe he became disillusioned, I don't know."

We reached the university. The large front doors were opened wide and we stepped inside. Not knowing where to find our professor Flavio asked one of the guards who directed us to the other side of a beautiful inner courtyard, filled with flowers and an ornate fountain, and up the stairs to an arched promenade on the second floor. There were students and teachers milling around and we asked a young man to direct us to the professor's office. He kindly led the way to the far end of the arcade and rang a small bell and almost immediately the professor opened the door and greeted us warmly.

We entered a rather cramped wood-paneled room with a high ceiling and hundreds of shelves of books. The professor directed us to two leather-bound chairs that sat in front of a large oak desk which was completely covered with files and books and papers, so much so that I thought it would have been impossible to find anything.

"Please sit down. Thank you for coming so quickly. I am sorry for that inconvenience but I must be in Milan tomorrow morning to lecture for a week. Milan would have been much farther for you and also I have my reference files here in this office. Please forgive me for just one moment."

He went to a corner of the room where several cabinets sat under the bookshelves and opened one, then returned carrying a thick overflowing file. He pushed aside some of the clutter on his desk to make room for it and sat down in his chair in front of us. He was still rummaging around for something as he said -

"You have set me to an extraordinary and difficult task, Signora, and in so doing I have become obsessed to the detriment of all my other work."

He finally found what he was looking for. His glasses. He put them on and continued as he opened the file and leafed through it.

"The symbols you have given me were most difficult to trace. They are certainly not Italian, or Roman, or Etruscan, nor any of the more ancient pagan symbols that we have usually found in Italy. No, they are even more distant than that."

"Where did they originate then?" I asked.

"That I do not know, not really. But from my research I have taken them as far back to six thousand years before the birth of Christ."

He pulled out a dog-eared paper, yellow with age, protected in a clear plastic sleeve.

"Here, I will show you."

He pushed the sleeve towards us. We looked at it. There was a lot of writing that meant nothing to me but there were two symbols drawn at the bottom of the page that I certainly did recognize.

"You see your symbols, yes?"

I nodded.

"Do you know, Signore," he said, turning to Flavio, "From where they originate?"

Flavio shook his head.

"That is what has amazed me. They originate from the Indus river valley in an area that is now primarily Pakistan but also partly India, Iran and Afghanistan. Here I will show you another document." He carefully removed another faded sheaf of paper, also sealed in a plastic sleeve. "You too will find it hard to believe, I think. It was kept under glass at an obscure church here in Florence where an old monk has sole responsibility for the book from which this page came and is the only one allowed to handle it. He also recognized the symbols, yes, and he opened the book to the exact spot. He graciously made me a copy, which I must return."

He paused, took off his glasses and placed them on top of his head.

"These are symbols of the Harappan, an ancient civilization that flourished in the valley from the ninth millennium before Christ. You may have heard of the great city of Mohenjo-Daro. There have been recent excavations in northwest India at a newly found site called Rakhigarhi and many important discoveries have been made. These symbols appear on many tablets and artifacts."

"How did they come to be pictured in the book in the church?" I asked.

"That is still a mystery, Signora. The monk would not show me the whole book."

"Do you know what the symbols mean?"

"Some could be mathematical. The Harappan civilization was advanced in every way, thousands of years before the Greeks."

"Was the monk willing to tell you anything about them?"

"Yes. He believes these symbols are similar to those found in another book."

"Which book?" Flavio asked.

"The unholy book of 'Vatra'. It is the book of vampires."

"Are you serious?" I exclaimed, throwing Flavio a look.

"Yes, I agree it is strange. The Harappan were not religious. There is no temple or deity of any kind depicted at the excavation site. But one thing that was found was curious. A cemetery. The bodies of the dead were buried not cremated, as was the custom throughout the entire Babylonian region, and carefully entombed in wooden coffins with their heads facing north and feet pointing south much like the legends of vampire burial. They may have believed in eternal life. There was found a seal with an engraving of a big-nosed man wearing a horned headdress. He is named the 'Lord of the Beasts' which suggests a cult. Female terracotta figurines from the latest excavation are described as pop-eyed and bat-eared which is unusual for a fertility symbol. The language itself has been only partly decoded. There is no source to find out for certain if these symbols are letters. Here is a sample from five tablets that were found buried beneath the city gates. The fact that some of the symbols are exactly what you found on your ceiling and on the papers in the box is remarkable considering we think this civilization died out completely more than a thousand years before the golden age of Greece. Did you ask the lady of the house where she got the tiles?"

"Yes. She said that, as far as she knew, they had always been there."

"I see. Fascinating, fascinating. But I am not sure I can be of any more help to you. You are welcome to take copies of these documents. I have drawn them as best I can. Here, I have made a file for you and, oh yes, here is the copper box. I found little information about it but it is probably no more than one hundred or one hundred and fifty years old. You could ask one of the coppersmiths in your town about that."

"Tell me more about the book of 'Vatra'."

"It is also believed to be Harappan in origin but, for myself, I truly doubt that the book of 'Vatra' exists."

We thanked the professor and Flavio spoke to him in Italian extending an invitation if ever he was back in our neck of the woods.

Outside the university again I felt a little light-headed and took a few deep breaths.

"Flavio, how could it be?"

"What, *carina*?"

"How could those symbols date back thousands of years before the birth of Christ?"

"It is not really a long time when you think how old mankind is."

"You know, Flavio, I'm embarrassed to admit it but when I saw Bela Lugosi as Dracula on the television when I was a little girl I slept with my window closed, even in the stultifying heat of summer, with the covers pushed up into my neck for fear that a vampire would come and bite me."

"The world is filled with many strange things," Flavio said with a smile, "Unless you can prove something does not exist, then until you do, it exists."

We arrived back in Montevecchio very late. The traffic was terrible. I realized I had run out of cigarettes so I asked Flavio to drop me at the bar in the old central square. He didn't want to but I assured him I would be fine. It was only nine o'clock.

"All right. But, *carina*, you will go straight home."

He looked out his window and scanned the bar and the square. It was empty except for the usual men playing cards.

"Oh, Flavio, we really must stop all this. From the minute I arrived in this town I've been convincing myself that there are strange goings on and that everything seems a little suspicious. I know the *carabinieri* are a bit frightening but on the whole the people have been very kind and helpful and I am not going to make myself paranoid any more. It's ridiculous. I'm perfectly fine. I may even have a brandy before I go home."

"It probably is not good to have too much imagination. *Bene*. Soon Marshall will be home and you can continue trying to become good Italians. *Ciao, carina*, but promise me you will not stay too long."

I just looked at him and smiled.

EIGHT

....

Inside the bar, Angelo greeted me with a familiar smile.

"Dov'è suo marito?"

"È a Roma. Ritorna la giorno dopo domani."

I then asked him for a pack of cigarettes. He asked me if I would like something to drink and I paused for a moment but then said, yes, I'd have a brandy. I sat quietly at the bar.

I took a sip of the drink. It tasted odd.

"Qual'è questo?" I asked.

"Un'aperitivo speciale!"

"È questa cognac?"

"Si, si. Molto buono. Piace bene il suo marito. Speciale."

"Oh, okay. *Io provo. Grazie."*

I took another sip. It was delicious. In truth, all the liqueurs we had tried in Italy were rather special and there were hundreds and hundreds of variations but nothing yet compared with Flavio's mother's walnut cordial. I nodded to Angelo that I liked it and he smiled and left me to myself and went over and began loading his small dishwasher.

I wasn't very comfortable drinking alone so I downed the *'aperitivo speciale'* in one big gulp and put a five euro note under the glass.

"*Grazie,* Angelo," I said.

One of the men got up and opened the door for me as I went out.

I wished him, *"Buona notte,"* and he smiled and tipped his

hat.

"Good evening, Signora," he replied.

When I got outside I looked up at the sky. It was filled with stars and the moon was almost full. I walked across the small square to the balustrade viewpoint and looked out over the valley. The sky was so bright I could see the outline of the distant mountains and the snow glistening on the tops. Lights twinkled for miles. It was *incantevole*. Enchantment. It was exactly that.

I took out a cigarette and lit it and started to feel dizzy. I realized I hadn't eaten anything much all day. Maybe the *aperitivo* was getting to me faster than usual and I regretted having it. Flavio was right, I should have gone straight home. I started walking down the laneway that led to the house when all of a sudden my knees buckled beneath me. I grabbed the wall but couldn't stop myself from falling. I hit the cobblestones and began to retch.

The events I will now try to describe are the reason I decided to write this story.

I thought I had fainted but felt myself being raised up and the weight of someone's arms against my body. Was I dreaming? I felt as light as though I were being carried away by the wind itself . . lifted away . . all the muscles in my body seemed to stiffen and I was unable to control them. I couldn't move. My eyes were open but I was numb, paralyzed. Then I felt a warmth come over my body and the sensation of being laid down gently onto a soft settee and I saw the most horrible sight.

The room was aglow. There was a fire burning. And all I could see were the bloody bulging eyes and swollen face and with only the dim flickering light upon him he appeared much larger and uglier than the monster on the stilts on the night of the *festa*. He could not have weighed less than four hundred pounds and his bulk was completely covered in a large colorful flowing caftan. His face was almost purple. The skin of his cheeks and forehead was stretched so tight it looked as though it could burst.

The walls were covered with photographs and images. There were sepia and black and white and the most recent were in color. They were obviously a pictorial history of this hideous being's life.

He was drinking something from a large flask. The liquid was deep red like the color of his skin. Was it blood? He swallowed the last of the contents and took up another flask and drank again without a pause.

A small hand was wiping my brow with a damp cloth. I caught sight of snow-white hair. It was the old woman looking down at me benignly. Her caress was kind and reassuring.

From somewhere behind her I could hear voices chanting.

"Strobor tek y bendem pury
Dli vit ids rom saltit
Noyo dar poro sangit vit
Sacara dur bet y corrli . . "

I couldn't understand the words but somehow their meaning became apparent as if by magic in my head. "We strive for purity in our life and for salvation. We sacrifice the blood for the good and the right."

I watched the creature as he finished the second flask. He paused and then began to speak. To my surprise his voice was melodic and pleasant but he had difficulty breathing which forced him to speak slowly.

"I am very sorry that it was necessary to drug you," he began, "But please do not be afraid. No one here will hurt you."

I tried to speak but couldn't.

"There is no need for words. I am able to listen to your thoughts. Are you comfortable?

"Good.

"You want to know why you have been brought here. A just question which I will answer in time.

"What you see before you is not my reality. I may look like a monster but that is only due to circumstance. In truth, I am a man of great intelligence and passion.

"You have become fascinated by our little village, have you not, Signora? Curious as to who we are and where we came from? And I hope you will bear with me. This is a most rare opportunity for me to meet someone like yourself who is from America. Interesting country. Very religious yet values freedom at any price. Fascinating dichotomy. And so I would like to give you a history of *my* people.

"We originated in what is now the Punjab province of northern Pakistan. Seven thousand years before the Athenians raised the Parthenon we were a sophisticated and technologically advanced urban civilization, more efficient and hygienic than many you might find in the modern world today. We had the first known sanitation systems with running water and covered drains and beautiful communal bathhouses. A delightful ritual banned by religious zealots everywhere.

"Having achieved new techniques in metallurgy and production of copper, bronze, lead and tin . . you have seen the beautiful artwork of this town . . our goods were famous all over Asia. We even had dentists who drilled teeth. It is true, Signora. The excavators found nine skeletons dating from eight thousand years ago with eleven drilled molar crowns. Besides razors, bronze mirrors and combs of ivory, we even had whistles, puppets and rattles for our children. Gambling was a favorite pastime. You are familiar now with the game *briscola* the old men play in the bars. We invented it.

"Our art and sculpture was beyond compare. We dug irrigation systems for our crops and we invented the plough. We practiced rainfall harvesting. We had massive reservoirs hewn from solid rock. We grew barley, cotton, peas, melons, wheat and dates. We had domesticated sheep and pigs, zebus and water buffalo.

"If the list is too long, Signora, it is only because I have great pride in the accomplishments of my race, that we were highly productive and capable of supporting a population of many millions without forced labor or slavery. That we had no kings, no armies, no priests, temples or palaces. Yet the archaeologists who have recently discovered our civilization are desperately searching for some sign of an oppressed society rather than an egalitarian, artistic and fundamentally self-principled one.

"You ask how does a race of millions reduce itself to a mere five hundred in a tiny hilltop village?

"It was not climate change nor an act of unearthly violence which annihilated our civilization in the second millennium before your Christ. In an inconceivably short time we became an infected race, a people who ceased to care about their cities, their lands, their harvests or even beauty. It came upon us suddenly . . the Vatra. Our people were no longer human as you know it. Yet one small group managed to escape.

"They traveled far and wide. They became vagabonds and horse dealers and they took with them their art of copper. They went from country to country but kept only to themselves until they reached a place where they felt they could at last begin again.

"That was almost five hundred years ago and in time they

were converted to the religion of the local people. Over the centuries when children were born with the sign of the Vatra there had only ever been one solution to the problem. It was necessary to kill them. But now the majority of the people found it against their newly found belief in the Catholic faith to commit such 'acts of mercy'. Therefore a small cabal secretly decided that one vampire had to exist to consume infected blood and I was chosen. It was a manner of death less easily detected than a wooden stake or silver pellet.

"You remember the legend of a man named Boro who was infected by Satan and driven from the town? That man was I. I have lived for five hundred years and all that time have made my home here as you see it. I have drunk countless flasks of unclean blood. And now you too have been chosen.

"Why? To become a vampire?

"No.

"To be my companion?

"Oh dear, no, no, not at all. I am sure you cannot imagine a more repulsive notion, though I confess, for me, it is a lovely thought.

"I have never left this room. I have never seen anyone except those few who hold my secret and are the guardians of my existence. I have never spoken English to anyone yet you see I am quite adept at the language. All these books have been brought to me over hundreds of years. I have a book on practically every subject.

"I have photographs to look at, some of which you will have noticed on the wall behind me, but it is not the same as seeing a snowfall in the late evening outside a window sparkling under the glow of the stars, a sunrise or a meadow filled with poppies, red heads raising their delicate bloom to the smiling sky above them. It has been centuries since I saw the sea or swam amongst the rolling waves, splashing water with the heat of the sun on my body.

"Our civilization once lived in the light of the earth's benevolence, in beauty and the procreation of beauty. Today they have God and so the earth has no relevance to them except for their use and destruction. Our people were told to celebrate the gifts of water, of barley, of flowers and animals. The earth was sacred, not man. Man was superior to nothing. Man was the basest element of the earth's profundity. Now man no longer has the power to hear the earth's breath and has lost the serenity of its stillness. Man must relearn what it means to be part of the mystery. The mystery is the joy. But instead of putting his arms around its beauty, believing in its sustenance and life-giving force, man created 'God', a malevolent dictator, an invisible tyrant that can make him genuflect, weep and despair at his lot in life on this wondrous planet, waiting endlessly for death and then eternal life, a black hole. Would it not be more intelligent for man to embrace what he sees rather than what he doesn't see? I have read all the books that inform one of the existence of God and after my study I knew that I had wasted my time. I used them for the fire which is both useful and beautiful, is it not?

"When we arrived in this village five centuries ago there were nine thousand inhabitants and we realized that it was almost impossible to control the spread of the infection so the gates of the village were strictly controlled. Many people who became suspicious of us and our ways fled the town and never returned and we were spurned by the surrounding population as other-worldly, not Italian, and that is the reason that today we number only five hundred.

"And now we come to why you, Signora, are here.

"Twenty years ago an infected baby born in this village was

not brought to me. It was given to a nun who had left her office. The woman had no idea what the consequence would be of such an act. She took the child to a far away seaside town and raised it as her own. She was found dead a few weeks ago and the manner of her death alerted us. We must find him. You see here in this newspaper another victim has fallen. We are afraid it may be impossible for us to capture him without exposing ourselves and revealing our secret and all that we have been trying so hard to achieve.

"Ah, you thought you had found a peaceful town in which to spend your retirement but I believe you have been sent to us. It is not a circumstance for the weak of spirit but, like me, you have been chosen for good reason.

"Christ, too, was chosen. Not that I think the allusion is apt. Jesus Christ has supplanted every other mad messiah for the last two thousand years. A remarkable feat for a man who talked to the air, who starved and tortured himself, who lived only in the company of men, men he loved and who loved him. A man who was vain enough to have himself crucified to prove to the world that what, he was immortal? He wanted to rise from the dead and walk the earth saving souls.

"And here am I. I too have triumphed over death and walked the earth saving souls. I too have had the power to change men and give them eternal life. Although I do not make water into wine, and magically feed thousands on five loaves and two small fishes, I have the power to feed you forever on a tiny drop of my blood. One bite on your body and I can make you immortal! Free of disease and despair! Released from fear!

"Isn't eternal life what Jesus tells the faithful to strive and pray for? Is that not what the church teaches? To eat the body and blood of Christ and enter eternity in Paradise? Then, as to redemption, how is he different from me? Why am I abhorred and not him? And the thousands that have come after him and in his name tortured and abused and slaughtered and suppressed? Those who have lived off the blood of mankind and kept them in ignorance and made fortunes from their misery? The Christ worshippers wish for heaven but have created a hell on earth. I prefer that mankind should enjoy this paradise.

"How easy it would be for me to kneel to the local priest and confess my sins. There would be forgiveness, indulgence, a sign of the cross, a little holy water, a rebirth to relieve me of my responsibility and give myself up to God. Then where would my people be? A little confessional and would I then be free? Would my people be free?

"Your kind would crucify me and then what? Another would come after me and infect the world and that would be the end of you. An Armageddon, you might say. The last judgment day when the undead will walk the earth into eternity. A wonderful and just ending for the so-called human species.

"But I, who have the power to unleash this horror on humanity, prefer to save it from such a tragedy. That is the difference between me and the righteous.

"You have the right and the freedom to choose what you wish to do. No one will harm you or disturb you if you do nothing. But we are all responsible for the future."

And just before I lost consciousness the last thing I saw was the old woman smiling down at me.

NINE

To say that I woke up the next morning not knowing how I got there would be an understatement. As I lay in my bed trying to remember the most unusual night in my life, the doorbell rang. I was beginning to hate the sound of that ring. I opened the shutters to see Flavio on my doorstep. 'Oh God, no,' I thought. I looked down and he saw me and said -

"You are still in bed? Are you well?"

"Oh, good morning. Just a minute, I'll let you in."

As I went downstairs, I had no idea what I was going to say to him. I opened the door.

"*Ciao*, Flavio."

He was his usual jolly self.

"I have brought my toothbrush."

"Oh, Flavio, I'm sorry, but I really don't feel well today."

"Why? What happened to you?"

"Oh, nothing really. I think I've got the flu. Please come in."

We went into the kitchen.

"Would you like some coffee?"

"No, *grazie*," he answered, "You did not sleep well?"

"No."

"Too much on your mind, I think."

"No, no, I'm just not feeling well."

"Here, let me see." He put his hand on my forehead. "Yes, you are warm. We must get you a doctor."

"No, I'll be all right."

And suddenly the doorbell rang yet again! I left Flavio and opened the door. The old woman smiled and handed me a package. Then she shook my hand and held it tightly.

Salve," she said.

I closed the door and hid the package in the umbrella stand.

"Who was that?" asked Flavio.

"Just kids. They like ringing the bell."

"Now, you go upstairs and get dressing and I will take you to the doctor. She is in the *centro*."

"No, really."

"Go. I insist. You look terrible."

I thought it was better to agree with him and then maybe I could convince him to go home. I dressed and we walked over to the clinic.

When we went in, there were quite a few people waiting and I noticed them all lower their eyes when they saw me. Flavio, of course, was unaware and kept chatting away which made me even more anxious. The doctor came out and walked directly to me and asked me in Italian what was wrong. Flavio spoke for me and said that I thought I might have the flu and she nodded and asked me to follow her. Flavio got up but she told him in perfect English that she didn't need him to interpret and led me into the consultation room.

"Please sit down," she said rather curtly.

"Thank you. I am so sorry . . "

She cut me off.

"We don't have much time. Only a few minutes."

I sat there stunned. How could she have known I was coming?

"You have been given a package?"

"Yes."

"Good. Open it. You will find a telephone number. He is waiting for your call. Do not worry, he speaks a little English. Now I will give you a prescription. When you go to the pharmacy for the prescription give the number to the chemist. He will make the call and you will wait while a meeting is arranged."

"Will I know who it is?"

"He will know you. I will tell your friend that all you need is rest and that he must leave you to do so and that I will look in on you later."

"He may want to stay with me."

"I will make sure that he goes home. Please send him in here."

I left the room and told Flavio the doctor wanted to see him.

"Okay, *carina,* but I don't like doctors."

He went into her office and I sat down for a few moments. The others in the room still avoided my glances and pretended to be occupied.

When Flavio came out he was all flustered and nervous.

"Oh, *carina!*" he said, once we were again in the street, "The doctor says I am quite ill. I have a big fever! I must go home immediately. She has given me these pills, antibiotics. Oh dear, I am so sorry, *carina.* Come, I will walk with you home. Do not worry, the doctor has assured me that you will be fine but she is not so sure about me! Come, I must go home to bed!"

"Yes, of course. I'm sure it is nothing serious."

"Oh, I feel terrible. I have such a headache. I am sorry, *carina,* that I cannot take care of you. What will Marshall think?"

"You must just get yourself home and don't worry about me. Call me tomorrow."

"Yes, yes, I will. If I can. *Ciao, ciao.*"

I went inside and took out the parcel and ripped off the wrapping paper. I opened the box of chocolates and found the piece of paper with the number written on it. I grabbed my purse and my jacket and, first making sure that Flavio's car was gone, made my way towards the pharmacy. I had no idea what to expect or even what would happen to me but I hadn't yet decided to go ahead with this bizarre scheme, time would tell. As I approached the pharmacy I kept looking around for anyone acting peculiar who might be the person I was supposed to make contact with but nothing seemed out of the ordinary.

I walked into the pharmacy. It was empty except for a young man having a prescription filled. I approached the chemist. I had no idea what to say and simply handed him the piece of paper. He smiled at me and went into the back of the shop. As I was waiting the young man left and an old man came in. The chemist returned with a little parcel and as he was handing it to me the old man reached over the counter and took it.

"Please you to stay here for five minutes," the chemist said, "Then walk past the *macelleria* and turn right at end of building. He waits for you there."

I nodded. As I waited several others came into the pharmacy. I pretended to look at the shelves and the perfumes, trying to seem unobtrusive. Then, as I glanced at the chemist, he tapped his wristwatch and said, *"Salve e grazie,"* and I smiled and left.

As I walked towards the butcher's, Marisa, the butcher's wife, waved to me and wished me good morning. The three other old ladies who always sat outside on her stoop greeted me warmly and asked me, as usual, if I was making *'una passeggiata'* on such a nice day. Yes, I told them. Then, of course, they asked where my husband was. Women did not perambulate on the streets unaccompanied. I told them he was visiting a friend.

I passed the shop and saw the alley between the buildings, where I turned right. Not far down a black Fiat Panda was parked by the stone wall. I got into the passenger seat and the old man started the car. We drove down the alley and turned left onto the road below which took us out of town.

We didn't speak for a long time. I kept wondering where he was going and finally realized we were heading for the mountains. The old man clearly felt my anxiety and gently patted my hand.

"We are soon," he said.

He drove us all the way up the steep winding road to the *rifugio,* the small chalet that sat half way to the top of the mountain of Sibilla. As we came up the last few hundred meters of the treacherous incline I wondered if the plan was simply to make me the bait for this being, this undead man, or if I was going to be his next victim.

As we neared the chalet the old man swung the car around into the back parking area. There was another Panda parked close to the building. We stopped beside the other car and the old man got out. He asked me to wait a few moments and disappeared into the *rifugio.*

I was quite frightened and kept checking to see if any creature might be lurking or if at any moment I might find myself at the business end of a pair of fangs. I didn't know if I was being watched or what to believe but soon the old man came out and opened the car door for me.

"Come, Signora," he said kindly.

As we entered the dining room I was completely shocked at what I saw. He was supposed to be sick and in bed but there he was sitting with his legs crossed, in all his usual pertness and affability. It was Flavio. I couldn't believe it.

"Flavio! What are you doing here?"

"I am truly sorry, *carina*. It must be a surprise to you, I know, but it had to be done this way."

"I don't understand. You're not the man they're looking for, are you?"

He got up and led me to a chair.

"I think you should sit down before you fall down. I will make you a strong espresso."

He went behind the bar and I sat in silence as he made the coffee.

"Drink that and I will try and explain," he said as he brought it to me.

I took the cup but my hands were shaking so badly I spilled some on the table.

Calma, calma, carina. "

"Flavio, I don't understand."

"I am not the man we are looking for. I am as mortal as you. But I must explain everything so you will understand and not be frightened. It was I who directed you to the professor and to the church and the underground passageway. It was I who locked us into the grotto."

"You! But why?"

"Wait. And it was I who finally brought you to Boro. I was there with you in that room. The drug we gave you made sure that your perceptions were a little inhibited, shall we say. It was I who told Boro that you were the one who could help us."

"But you said that you didn't know the town, that you had

never been there before except as a child with your classmates. Why did you lie to me?"

"It was necessary. I may have hinted at a few things but it was impossible for me to fully reveal myself to you."

"Then you come from my village?"

"Your village? Ah, *carina*, you are dear to me. You see? I was right. You are one of us."

"But Flavio . . "

"Please let me finish, then you will ask me questions."

"And so the doctor . . "

He cut me off.

"It is necessary to have professionals otherwise we could not do what we do. It would be impossible without a doctor to find out if someone is contaminated or not. We do not live in the 3rd century, *carina*. We cannot go around eliminating the diseased without evidence and justification. We are in need of those who can help. I am in that position also."

He took out a cigarette and lit it and offered me the pack.

"You don't smoke."

He laughed.

"And so I don't. Now be quiet. I know how hard that is for you."

He laughed again. I was beginning to feel reassured that he might still be the same old Flavio.

"When you first came to Le Marche and we met I did not know that you would be the one. When you asked me for help because you and Marshall were a little worried, and not sure of yourself about the house you were buying, I knew that I had the opportunity to make you trust me and take you into a friendship."

"So this is the only reason you became my friend?"

"At first, but it did not take long to fall under your spell and I knew then that you would be the one to help us. It was easy to convince the others. They too felt that you were different. You were kind and full of enthusiasm, eager to understand our people and our culture. So we agreed. But now you want to know for what purpose you have been chosen. This is very difficult for you, I am sure. You did not expect this to be part of your Italian dream."

"But why me? Why not you or someone else from the town?"

"It cannot be me, *carina*. You see, I am infected."

I looked at him and couldn't believe what he was saying.

"Yes, *mia cara*, I am allowed to function normally only because of transfusions. I will explain. I am the son of a vampire and a mortal woman. The man my mother is married to now is not my real father. She met him after I was born."

"Then who is your father?"

"The man who lived in the castle."

"Your great-uncle?"

"Yes. But my mother is completely unaware of this. She had no idea what he was and still does not know."

"Then your uncle is alive."

"No. He has been taken care of. But you must listen to me, *carina*, and not ask so many questions. I am what they call a 'damphir'. One who is born of a vampire and a mortal woman. 'Damphir' have one power only and that is to be able to detect signs of vampirism. There have been times in the past when 'damphir' were created amongst our people because there was need of them. I was such a birth."

My mind was reeling.

"Oh, Flavio, but that is terrible, just terrible."

"We must all carry some responsibility in this world but, like the others when their work is done, I too will be allowed to pass into peaceful death."

Even though I had known him for only a few months I loved him as though he was my brother. At that moment I realized that after this nightmare was over I might never see him again and I began to weep.

"No, no, I do not want your tears. I want your courage. I will have served my people and that is enough for me. I do not wish anything to do with eternity. One life is enough. Now, listen to me. What I am going to ask you to do is dangerous but I promise you that nothing will happen to you if we can help it. Do you still agree?"

"Yes, now more than ever," I said softly, my confidence returning.

"That is better," he said and took my hand. "Remember when I showed you my uncle's castle? I brought you there on purpose so you would be seen by him."

"But you told me your uncle was dead."

"Not my uncle, the one we are looking for now. I wanted you to go walking alone in the woods. I thought maybe then he would be lured to come out but he never appeared."

"You were there?"

"Of course. Do you think I could let you walk alone near the undead?"

"But I saw him! Or I thought I saw him."

"No, it was your imagination. He has escaped into the mountains."

He reached over and the old man handed him the packet he had taken from me at the chemist's. He carefully unwrapped it. In it was a syringe full of clear fluid.

"We do not use stakes or silver bullets or crosses anymore. They are too easy to trace and a terrible way for the undead to suffer. Before the infected blood has time to poison the entire body we simply stop its spread with this drug. Afterwards at the crematorium we finish the work by draining the blood and then we take the contaminated blood to Boro. The body is then burned and the ashes thrown into the holy lake of Sibilla at the top of the mountain. This boy must not fall into the hands of the authorities or anyone outside our village. You remember the newspaper report you showed me? Once the authorities find a body before us there is nothing we can do. We have to steal it from the cemetery to make sure it will not rise again. That is why secrecy is of the utmost importance. In order to explain exactly why you are the one we need I must put to you a few personal questions."

"That depends on how personal."

"Nothing that you will feel ashamed to answer."

"Okay."

"Firstly, you wear glasses, yes?"

I nodded.

"Do you have good hearing?"

"Excellent. Sometimes I wish I was deaf. I can hear a conversation from the other side of a crowded room."

"Are you sensitive to light?"

"I don't think so. I never wear sunglasses no matter how brilliant the light is."

"Do you get ill often?"

"As a matter of fact, I rarely get sick."

"Do you have an extra rib?"

"Yes, I do. Funny, how do you know that?"

"Never mind. You have only one child?"

"Yes, I've never taken any contraceptives but we only managed to have one child."

"Did the doctor give you something when you were pregnant?"

"Yes. It was terrible. A large needle. He said I needed it because my blood and my baby's weren't compatible."

"So then he must have told you that you were of a rare blood type?"

"No. I've forgotten what type he said I was. It was years ago. What is all this, Flavio?"

"What if I told you that you had a blood type so rare that it exists in only one in four million people."

"You're kidding."

"Not at all. It is called Bombay blood. But it was once called copper blood."

"What do you mean, do I have copper in my blood?"

"It is very true. Your blood has a very high ratio of copper. Why do you not wear a watch?"

"Because they just . . stop. They never last very long."

"You never wear any jewellery."

"No, I'm allergic. I can't even wear my wedding ring."

"Your blood type has been traced back to 30,000 years ago. It cannot be cloned. You cannot receive blood from just anyone and yet you can give your blood to everyone. Strange, no?"

I laughed.

"Yes . . "

"With blood like yours you are resistant to most disease, even HIV."

"Impossible."

"No, it is documented."

"And?"

"And that is why I come to the reason you are the only one to help us."

I let him continue even though I found the whole thing difficult to believe.

"The blood type found in the Indus civilization was 100% 'copper blood'. RH negative. It is obvious your ancestry is from there."

"I don't think so."

"Never mind, it is so. The boy is diminishing in strength due to the fact that his own blood cells are being attacked from the blood he has lived on so far. He needs a host body to feed on that is of his type and healthy and disease resistant. For him to find such a single human being would take a lifetime and he would inevitably become ghostlike and that would be horrible to him. He wants to be a god, a powerful being, not a sickly pale skeleton. So his own vanity has forced him to find his 'mate'. He will choose you. I have no doubt. His keen sense of smell will recognize you."

I gulped.

"He already has, I think."

"What do you mean?"

"If it is who I think you are talking about, he was the boy who danced with me the night of the disco."

"*Ai, mio Dio!* And at that moment I left you unprotected to have a pee."

He took my face in his hands.

"O, *mia cara*, I am deeply sorry."

I shivered slightly.

"Why did he not take me then?"

"I do not know," he said softly. "If you do not want to do this I will understand and it will never change the way I feel about you."

It would be a lie to say I wasn't terrified but I knew I had to make up my mind and had only a few moments to do so.

"I think we will leave you alone to think about it," he said quietly.

He got up and put his arm around the old man's shoulders and they left the room.

As I sat there looking out the window, taking in the beautiful view of these marvelous mountains, I thought about Marshall and my family. No matter what Flavio had said to reassure me there was always the chance that I too would become infected. It would mean the end of my life. As I sat there weighing the consequences of my decision Flavio came back into the room.

"*Cara?*"

I looked at him and he smiled. He knew what I was going to say.

"You know you will not ever be able to tell Marshall what you have done or that you have seen 'him'. This is one secret you will have to keep and take to your grave. That I think will be the most difficult thing of all."

"Yes, you are probably right. But before we go, Flavio, I need to ask *you* one question. Did you have anything to do with Michael's accident?"

"Ah, that was unfortunate. Your friend had wanderlust it seems and that night after he left an apartment of a woman he had been with he collapsed. We had been following him throughout his stay because we were worried about his obsessive filming. We called the doctor who revived him and we drove him to the *centro* where you found him."

"Why didn't you take him to the hospital?"

"Because there was nothing they could do. He was gravely ill and had not long to live. We believed it was best for him to return to England."

"Are you telling me the truth?"

Flavio leaned across the table and again took my hand in his.

"Yes. I could not wish any harm to come to a friend of yours."

"So you have the camera."

"Yes. I can return it to you. But there is no film."

"No, I don't want it."

He called the men back in.

"She is ready."

He took the packet from the old man and handed it to me.

"You must keep this with you at all times. It will paralyze him, nothing more, until we can deal with him. There is an ancient ruin in a high valley under the mountain of Sibilla where we believe he is living. It is a long walk, maybe six kilometers through rough terrain. These men will take you only as close as they think it is safe without being detected. There you will have to go on alone."

He took something out of his pocket. It was a small revolver. He handed it to me.

"For your safety. Use it if you have to. The men are armed and also have a vial just in case."

I took the gun and put it in my pocket.

"Now you will go with them."

He spoke to the men in rapid-fire Italian and shook them all by the hand, then came to me and bent down to kiss me on both cheeks.

"They will not fail you. I will see you when it is done."

He left me sitting there. I held the gun in my hand. I had never fired a shot in my life. Finally I forced my legs to stand up and walked over to the men who were to be my protectors and they led me out of the chalet to where and what I had no idea.

TEN

....

We drove over a winding dirt road as far as it took us and then the rest of the journey was on foot. It was a very long trek and I wasn't in the best of shape. At one point, near a rushing river, the men told me to sit down and rest. They brought me water and some bread and cheese. All I could think of when I looked at the sandwich was Flavio saying, "No cheese!", and I smiled.

We rested for about fifteen minutes and, as I looked out over the lush valley, I felt a little sadness, knowing I would never see it again.

The last few hundred yards were very steep and craggy. I was surprised that I could do it and my vertigo had all but disappeared. We approached the top of the mountain and the men pointed in the distance to a ruined tower beyond a small forest. They checked that I had not lost the vial and revolver. They hugged me and said, *"Salve"*, then they turned to head up the other direction towards the tower.

Once I entered the wooded area there was no turning back. A veil of darkness descended and it was difficult to maneuver through the bracken. After about a hundred metres or so I came to a clearing and the ruins and the great tower stood before me. He must be in there. No sooner had I thought it than I heard a high-pitched, light and almost monotone voice speaking to me.

"Good day, Signora."

My heart leapt into my throat. I spun around and there he was standing on top of a pile of rocks. He shimmered in the sunlight. He wore a long black coat and his hair was dark. His skin was as pale as diamond. I thought he was the most beautiful being I had ever seen, tall and slim and luminescent. I was transfixed by the sight of such beauty. His smile was radiant as he gazed down at me and spoke again.

"You are not as young as I thought. I saw you in the darkness. I am sorry. I am a little selfish. I hoped you would be much younger and much more beautiful. But one must be satisfied with what one is given. I have watched you from afar in that village of mine where the people are stupid and ignorant. God will save them? They will all go to heaven if they live like sheep and pray on their knees? And they will have eternal life? There is no eternal life with God. The only way is through me."

I tried to speak but I couldn't.

"The lies those men of God have sold to mankind. They would prefer to die and be buried in the dirt, never to exist again. I will change this and you will help me, Signora. You and I together will bring release to my people."

I was still completely unable to move. He came ever closer and I could only feel my heart pounding in my chest as he raved.

"I will free my people, not him! It is I who have power now. He cannot stop me. It was unfortunate I had to wait so long but once you and I are one and our blood has mixed together then we will infect the others and bring them glory."

Suddenly he flew into the air and disappeared and in a split second he was behind me, his arms locked around my body. I could feel his breath on my neck and he whispered in a liquid voice -

"Be not afraid. You will live forever in this glorious world, never to feel hunger or cold or pain, and I will not be lonely. No love, no hate, just pleasure. You must admit that pleasure is the only real human emotion that leads to happiness."

He turned me towards him and I looked into those brilliant deep pools of blue. I knew there was no escape.

"You are so beautiful," I murmured.

He laughed.

"I know, and when I am fully undead I will be so for eternity. This is my gift to you, Signora. Now you may speak. I know what he has told you but you tell me why we should not live here in this beautiful place together."

I could feel the blood running through my veins again but I had no idea how to answer his question.

"Speak! You must admit that to live here forever would be better than any heaven God could give you."

My voice was hoarse as I formed a reply.

"Since I don't believe in God it is difficult for me to answer your question."

"Ah, I see. You do not believe in God or you don't believe in eternal life."

"I don't believe in either," I said quietly, "You say a gift. What is this gift? To live with you in an endless wasteland preying on others. To know that one is dying the minute one is born is the only thing that gives life meaning."

"How can you leave all this beauty willingly?"

"To leave it is one thing. The fact that it will never leave me is eternal. I wouldn't trade that for anything, not God, not you or your so-called paradise."

Suddenly his face, his beautiful face, became distorted and his eyes turned black and his mouth turned thin and cruel. Then he flew to the very top of the ruined tower and pressed his head into his hands and looked up at the sky and let out a howl so piercing that I could feel it shake my own soul.

"IT IS NOT ENOUGH!!!!" he screamed to the heavens.

I quickly looked around for the men. It was the only moment I would have to make a run for it. I tried to but he held me with his gaze. Again I could not move. I tried to shout to the men for help but again I had no voice. He shimmered and it was as though he was lifted into the air as gracefully as a floating balloon and landed in front of me. I tried to reach for the syringe but my body was frozen. He held me in his power. I felt as though I was being sucked into deep pools of clear water. I felt myself relax, as though I wanted to be consumed and drawn even deeper into them, letting go of all thought and feeling, floating free of all emotion and pain, a state of perfect euphoria, like a drug I was given once in the hospital . . like giving up my life.

I have no memory of what happened next except that when I regained consciousness I was lying on the ground in the sunshine and there was no one there. I slowly got to my feet and looked around. I called to the men. I looked for him. I searched the ruins but there was no one. I felt dizzy and frightened. I checked my body, my neck especially, but there was no blood, not even a scratch. I checked for the packet but it was gone and so was the gun. It could have been a dream for all anyone knew. They had left me there alone and I realized I would have to make the return journey without them.

As I walked away from the ruins and out of the wood I turned back to make sure no one was following or watching me but everything looked so peaceful and somehow I knew the young man was no longer there.

When I finally got back to the spot where we had left the car it was getting dark and there was no one waiting for me and the car was gone. What were they thinking? It was miles more down the stony winding road to the *rifugio* but there was little I could do so I began walking.

I walked on until nightfall and then saw the headlights of a vehicle coming up towards me. I ran and waved at the driver but as it neared it halted and started turning round. I kept yelling and waving, running as fast as I could to reach it. Then it stopped. 'Thank God,' I thought. I came up to the car and there he was, sitting in the driver's seat, all smiles and pert as usual.

"Carina."

It was the only word he spoke as he helped me into the jeep and that was the last time I ever saw Flavio.

When Marshall returned from Rome the next day after his meeting with the publisher he was elated. Signor del Credi wanted to publish his novel and to acquire any more that he may have written.

"Well, that's wonderful," I said.

Then he explained to me that the state of Michael's health had been more serious than even he had thought and that he actually died of an embolism. There was no need to be interviewed by the *carabinieri* because the London police had sent them an affidavit as to the cause of death.

"Marshall?"

"Yes?"

"I think I want to go home."

"Of course, we have a flight to go back in October but we may have to change that if I sign a contract with del Credi."

"No, I mean now."

"What?"

"I mean I want to go home for good."

"Are you serious? We just bought this house. We won't be

able to sell it for years. You know what the Italians say, 'is easy to buy, is very difficult to sell'!"

"I know, but we really don't belong here. We'll never be part of them, we'll always be *stranieri*. No matter how hard we try we're not Italian."

"Why this change all of a sudden?"

"Oh, I don't know. I guess I miss our life back home."

My eyes had welled up with tears and Marshall noticed.

"But what about my publisher?" he said gently.

"You can send him books from anywhere, can't you?"

"But I wanted to die here."

"Please don't talk about death."

"But this is ridiculous! You love it here? What about your dear friend Flavio?"

Yes, what about Flavio?

"Oh Marshall, wouldn't it be wonderful if he could come to visit us in America?"

Just then the doorbell rang.

"I'll get it," Marshall said, "I bet it's the old lady across the way with more chocolates."

He opened the door and I heard the voice of our estate agent, Elena.

"I am so sorry to bother you. I hope I do not disturb you."

"No, no, not at all," answered Marshall, "Please come in."

They came into the kitchen. There was another woman standing behind her. It was the lady I had been introduced to at the café, whose family had once lived here. I had completely forgotten I had agreed to show the house.

"This is Signora Garafaldi. This is unusual, I know, but the Signora is asking if you would like to sell your house."

Marshall was stunned but I quickly chimed in.

"Please sit down. Would you like some coffee?"

Of course I knew who had sent her.

We were offered a very good price for both the house and all the contents and we accepted. Marshall was rather upset but I convinced him that it was a deal we couldn't refuse and that we could return any time to visit this beautiful and strange country.

And he never pressed me, really pressed me as to why I wanted to abandon our dream of a home abroad and for that I am grateful because I made a promise to a friend. It may be the only one I have ever truly kept in my life.

Until now.

ACKNOWLEDGEMENTS

I would like to thank my husband, Alan Scarfe and daughter, Tosia Scarfe, for keeping me tied to my chair while I wrote my first novella. I would also like to thank the wonderful people of the beautiful hilltop town that inspired it.

Thank you to Aaron Rachel Brown for her cover design, Patrick Hughes for his wonderful photographs, and to my editor, Heidi von Palleske, at Smart House Books.